Flying With Prayer

RB Parkline

Published by RB Parkline, 2020.

FLYING WITH PRAYER

First edition. June 16, 2020.

Copyright © 2020 RB Parkline.

ISBN: 978-1393954088

Written by RB Parkline.

Flying with Prayer

Chapter I

The small Cessna airplane shook in the turbulence. Frankie closed her eyes, gripping the arm rest tightly. Tony looked at her smiling, "just turbulence." Frankie tried to smile as she stared out the front window. She had flown many times, but not on a smaller plane. She looked out the side window seeing the landscape passing quickly under her. She thought about how it looked like a monopoly board. She breathed in deep, gaining control of her emotions. Thinking to herself everything was going to be okay, Tony after all was an engineer, as well as an astronaut. He worked for NASA, and had been to the International Space Station. She smiled as she looked at Tony in the pilot's seat. She saw him looking at the control panel then glanced at her.

"We will be landing in about ten minutes."

She smiled thinking how nice he looked, and he seemed at ease at the controls of the small four seat plane. Speaking through the microphone of his headset. She was also wearing a headset so they could speak.

"Now you will like my family, and they will love you." He hesitated. "They're pretty ordinary, but my Mother is, well she is unconventional."

Frankie smiled knowing Tony was attempting to prepare her for meeting his family. She thought of him meeting her family. She almost laughed thinking about unconventional, her family defined the word unconventional.

Tony spoke to the airport in Salem Oregon preparing to land. The Cessna began its descent. With the runway in sight Tony brought the plane down softly as the wheels touchdown. He slowed the plane then headed off the main runway towards the hangers. When he stopped Frankie removed her headset stepping out of the plane. She saw a tall man walking towards them.

Tony reached in the back taking out two suitcases along with a smaller bag. Walking around the plane He saw his Dad walking towards them. The man smiled as he looked at the tall beautiful woman in front of him.

"You must be Frankie?"

Yes, I am."

"John Pierce," He said hugging her tightly. His strong arms embracing her. He stepped back looking at Tony. "That was a nice landing son."

"Thanks Dad," Tony said shaking his hand. "Mom didn't come with you?"

John reached over taking a suitcase. "No, you know your Mother she would have a panic attack seeing you land that plane." He continued to smile as he looked at Frankie "April has a few issues, and one of them is flying.

Frankie smiled as she looked at the big man who was over six feet tall. He was not what she expected. He was tall, with broad shoulders, long powerful arms, with dark hair, and a moustache. Tony was not as tall, being five nine, with a small build. She was the same size as Tony. She was five nine with an athletic build. Dark brown hair down to her shoulders, and brown eyes.

They walked into the airport building where a man taller than Tony grinning came out of an office. "Welcome home space cadet!"

Tony laughed taking his hand, "good to see you Joey."

They talked for a while, Tony introduced Frankie to Joey who he had gone to school with.

They walked out of the airport to a Ford F one fifty. Tony placed the suitcase in the back, then walked to the passenger side. He stopped seeing Frankie step into the front seat. He opened the door to the back seat stepping in. John looked at Frankie then to Tony in the back seat. He smiled as he started the pickup backing up.

John maneuvered the pickup through traffic which was light. Frankie looked out the window "Salem is nice."

John nodded as he stopped at a traffic light. "It's growing."

"How's work going," Tony asked from the backseat as he stared out the window seeing the town which had not changed."

"Good, Mental Health is adding on so we're stringing wire today."

"Maybe Bevis, and Butthead can get some counseling while they're working."

John turned to look at Tony then looked back.

"You're Mother is irritated with you since you missed her birthday."

"I sent her an email."

John looking straight ahead said "that doesn't count, A card written on with a pen, envelope, with a stamp." he looked at Frankie. "April is old fashioned."

Feeling the tension, Frankie smiled "I told Tony he should get his Mother a card."

"She's making that up."

John laughed as he drove.

Leaving the city, they turned on a two lane road then after two miles turned on a gravel road. When John turned into a driveway with a large mailbox she saw the house. It was a large two story log cabin with a porch. She saw a woman in a rocking chair stand up.

John followed the circle drive stopping in front of the log cabin. Frankie, and Tony stepped out of the pickup. Frankie watched as the woman holding onto the rail made her way down the steps. She was a smaller woman Five four, with a small build. Her long, light blond hair with streaks of grey in a ponytail tied back which came to her waist. She was wearing a white blouse with short sleeves, a long skirt which was floral print, with sandals. She had on a pair of large round glasses. She walked up to Frankie hugging her neck. She stepped back holding both Frankies hands, "I'm April, so you will call me that. It is so good to meet you Frankie." She looked at Frankie intently then dropping her hands walked to Tony hugging him. "I'm so glad you came home honey."

Tony hugged her "Glad to be here Mom."

He took the suitcase from the back of the pickup. Frankie picking up the smaller bag. Holding Frankies hand they walked to the cabin; April dropped her hand grasping the rail. "You need to hold the rail honey."

Frankie moved the small bag to her right hand lightly touched to rail as she walked up the five wooden steps, followed by Tony, and John.

April opened the door as they walked inside. John sat the suitcase down.

"I need to get back to work. I'll see you tonight." He turned walking outside, shutting the door behind him.

Frankie looked at the large open room which was filled with a couch, and chairs. She could see a long table with chairs in the back. A nice fireplace of stone.

"This is really nice. Tony said you lived in a log cabin, I didn't imagine it was so big."

April glanced over her shoulder at Tony. She took Frankies hand walking toward the staircase leading to the second level.

"Oh I'm sure Tony led you to believe it was a one room cabin with a big pot hanging in the fireplace." She looked back at Tony as she started up the steps. "Use the handrail honey."

Frankie tried not to laugh as she touched the sturdy wooden rail.

"Now the bedrooms are up here." She pointed to a door as they walked. "You can put your suitcase in your room Tony." She continued to walk as Tony sat the two suitcases down opening the door. They moved to another door which she opened.

"This is Sissy's old room. I hope you will be comfortable."

Frankie looked at the daybed with a yellow print quilt. "This is nice," she said, sitting the small case on a dresser drawer.

"April took her hand, speaking softly "I think it would be appropriate for you to sleep in here. I, well I," she hesitated as she looked away. "I don't know how close you, and Tony." She stopped as she looked anxiously up at Frankie.

"We're not sleeping together."

April smiled shyly."I wasn't implying, I mean, well we are Methodist, and, and." She stopped talking as she sat on the daybed.

Frankie sat next to her. "I understand, and appreciate you not assuming we are intimate."

April was nervous, "Oh my, I would never, I mean, I know you are a woman, and, and you are very beautiful, and Tony is well I believe he is handsome.'

Frankie tried not to laugh knowing April was nervous.

"Actually I was raised in Church."

"I'm so happy to hear that. What Church do you attend?"

"Penacostal."

"Penacostal! Oh, well they are quite enthusiastic. Well I hear anyway.

"They can get enthusiastic, at times."

April looked intently at Frankie, "do you speak in tongues?" She spoke just above a whisper.

"No, I do not have that gift. My Mother does at times speak in the Angels language."

April stared at Franke, she stood up slowly "OK then, well I suppose the Holy Ghost does bestow gifts."

Tony walked in carrying a suitcase sitting it next to the dresser. April walked to him hugging his neck.

"It's been too long since you came home Tony."

"I know, and I am sorry Mom."

"You forgot my birthday."

"I sent you an email."

She looked at him shaking her head. "Yes I did get it, It was cute, but it's not a card."

"I'm sorry, I'll send a card next year."

"Well I have to get back to the shop, Sissy will need help. I will see you tonight, Your Father will be grilling." She smiled looking at Tony, and Frankie. "Your brother's with their families will be here, as will Sissy, and Dean with the twins."

She walked out with Tony, and Frankie following her.

Tony showed her the other bedrooms as well as the rest of the house. They walked out the back two double French doors to a large patio which was wood. They walked down the steps.

"Mom has an issue with heights, It's not a phobia, she just wants people to be safe."

"So we should use the handrail." Frankie said giggling.

"Got itl"

In the large backyard were two huge green houses. Tony opened the gate leading out of the large yard. He stopped as a large Rottweiler came running towards them. Tony held out his hand as the large dog stopped. He sniffed Tony's hand as he growled low. The dog looked up at Tony as he patted him under his chin. He stepped back, taking Frankie's hand holding it in front of the Rottweiler. As he sniffed her hand Tony speaking quietly said "Rufus guards the greenhouses."

Frankie gently stroked the large dog's back.

She followed Tony to a greenhouse with Rufus close beside her.

Inside the greenhouse Frankie was amazed at the number of plants. Tony explained his Mother raised herbal plants. She had raised plants before it was popular. "She was ahead of her time. Now everybody uses essential oils."

Frankie thought of her Mother who believed in essential oils. They were of course natural oils extracted from plants.

"Everything is organic, all natural. No pesticides, or chemicals allowed. The fertilizer is all natural, chicken poop from a local farmer."

Walking through the greenhouse which was filled with plants Frankie was in awe. She jumped when water began to spray on her;

Tony laughed, taking her hand. "Automatic sprinklers, they're set on a timer."

Frankie giggled as they walked out of the greenhouse to the other greenhouse.

Frankie was surprised as she looked at the plants in the greenhouse. It was filled with marijuana. Holding her hand Tony walked down the narrow aisle of the tall marijuana plants.

"Mom is a licensed grower here in Oregon. The state passed medical, and recreational marijuana. Mom has always believed marijuana has medicinal value. More so than what drugs pharmaceutical companies make. She extracts the oil, and sells it to other dealers. She does sell to distributors who sell it for recreational purposes, she doesn't approve, but she does make good money."

The smell was overwhelming as Frankie looked at the marijuana.

"So that is why Rufus is on duty, to guard the marijuana."

"Yes, no one wants to steal aloe vera, or honeysuckle plants."

They walked into the house where Tony poured them a glass of tea. He explained how his mother was now legal with raising marijuana.

"There was a time she grew it as medicine. She did not sell it to heads who wanted to get high."

"Heads" Frankie asked, confused.

"Pot heads."

Frankie sipped her tea smiling. "And the tea is organic."

"Of course."

Chapter II

The family gathered on the back patio. Tony's brothers were older, and big like their Father. Ricky with his wife Janice, and three sons, Bobby with his wife Helen, their two sons, and a daughter. Sissy whose name was June, with her twin daughters, and baby girl. John poured charcoal into the large grill.

"We use charcoal, which is more natural, and it just makes the meat taste better. We don't use gas in this house."

"Now John there's nothing wrong with using gas." April looked nervously at Frankie.

"My Dad's the same way. Why use gas, might as well just cook in the house."

"He's a wise man."

April shook her head looking at John "Men." She took the baby from Sissy holding her close. "So Tony said you worked at a hospital in Houston. You're a nurse?"

"A Nurse Practitioner, which means I can write prescriptions."

"I didn't know nurses could write prescriptions? I thought Doctors had to do that," Janice asked curiously.

"I received my RN license while I was in the Marine Corps. A Doctor I worked with in Afghanistan encouraged me to go for my practitioner licenses. So I decided to go for it when I left the Corps. I decided to stay in the reserves."

"A Marine," Ricky said. "Well I'm glad to hear that. I've been worried 'bout Tony in Houston alone. Now he has someone to protect him!"

Bobby, and Ricky both laughed.

"He could get a serious paper cut sitting at his desk" Bobby said as he laughed.

"Good to have a nurse to stop the blood flow." Rick snickered.

"Enough" April said, shaking her small finger at Ricky, and Bobby. She looked at John who looked at the two boys laughing.

Frankie watched as Tony sat quietly looking at his two brothers. He stood up walking to the backyard where the children were playing. He caught a frisbee thrown to him then threw it back.

"You served in Afghanistan, Ricky asked?"

"Three tours."

Ricky looked intently at her "I served two tours, and Bobby served two, Airborne Rangers. Tony served three tours."

"Air Force" Bobby said "must have been tough in the airplane, above all the action"

"So how did you meet," Sissy asked, leaning forward looking at Frankie.

Frankie was looking at Ricky, and Bobby, she felt the anger rising hearing the insult about Tony. She fought her emotions, wanting to explode. She looked at Sissy, sipped her ice tea. "It was at church."

April smiled "what church do you attend?"

Frankie was still angry looking at April, "it's a nondenominational church. It's actually a Mega Church." She wanted to add "Don't worry it's not a Pennicostal Church." She saw the nervous look on April's face as she held the small baby tight."

"I'm glad you are attending," she said as she looked down at the baby.

Frankie took a deep breath letting it out slowly. "I had lived in Houston for about four months before I went. I work ten hour shifts. So when my shift changed I was able to go. I was sitting in Sunday school which was a huge class. It was for singles. I saw this good looking man come in. He walked over, and sat next to me. He was staring at me so I turned, and looked directly at him. He asked "are you ok, I hope it didn't hurt when you fell from heaven?" The group all laughed. "So I said a little."

John smiling said "Hamburgers done."

April stood up going to the end of the table. She picked up the hand sanitizer, and as each family member walked by she squirted some in their open hand. Each took a hamburger with the lettuce, tomatoes and pickles on the table. The children were fed first as the adults followed.

Sitting at the table Sissy holding her hamburger asked "so what did you think of Tony's cheesy line?"

"I thought it was cute. So he of course followed me into the sanctuary sitting next to me." She looked at Tony putting her hand on his shoulder "He was cute, and charming."

"Takes after his Father." April said as she looked at John who smiled.

"Did he ask you out?" Janice asked.

"He did, but I told him no. I went to church that evening, and was sitting by myself when Tony came in, and sat next to me. After the service he invited me out for ice cream."

"Ice cream oh that has so much sugar in it Tony." April said frowning.

"Actually it was yogurt." Tony said looking at his Mother.

"Yogurt!" Bobby laughed. "Did you get sprinkles on it?"

"Blackberries," Tony said looking at Bobby.

"Probably wearing the pink polo, didn't get any yogurt on it did you?"

Tony looked at Ricky without speaking.

"Stop it, both of you, just stop it!" April stood up, her two fists Clenched. "You wonder why Tony never comes home, and, and." Tears coming down her cheeks walked off.

"I'm sorry Mom we were just giving the kid a hard time." Rick said as he watched April walk off.

Frankie temper was flaring as she stared at Ricky, and Bobby. Leaning over said in a low growl. "You won't think it's so funny when I break your jaw. Don't worry I'm a nurse so I will patch you back up."

"Sit back Frankie." She looked at John looking at her. You're a guest."

He looked at Ricky, and Bobby. "I'll kick both of their butts." The anger in his face was apparent.

Frankie sat back, she glanced at Tony who sat quietly.

John leaned forward "you upset your Mother."

Janice looked at Ricky "It's like this everytime. You just can't keep your mouth shut."

Ricky stood up as did Bobby going into the house. The rest of the group sat quiet. Frankie sipped her tea. She was furious. She took a deep breath trying to control her temper which was about to spin out of control.

April walked out of the house followed by Ricky, and Bobby.

"I'm sorry for offending you Tony." Ricky said as he sat down."

"Sorry Tony."

April wiped her eyes, she looked up then said "you did go out on a date with Tony?"

Frankie nodded her head glaring at Ricky, and Bobby who were not looking at her.

"I was at the hospital when I received a phone call." She looked at Tony smiling "He called me at work to let me know he had tickets to the Huston Astros ball game on Saturday. So on Saturday morning he came to my house on his Kawasaki."

"A motorcycle, you still have that motorcycle Tony?" April said, looking at her son."

"It was a nice day for a ride."

"Motorcycle's are so dangerous. I thought you got rid of it when you left Stanford."

Tony shrugged his shoulders.

Frankie smiled, putting her arm on Tony's shoulder. "He handed me a helmet. I put it on, and stepped onto the bike in the driver's seat."

The group laughed as April stared at Frankie.

"I held my hand out for the keys, and Tony stood there with his helmet on staring at me. He handed me the key, and got on the back."

"I had to put my arms around her waist to hang on. I wasn't sure of her driving."

"Of course" John said "safety has to come first."

The group at the table giggled.

"We arrived at the game, and the seats were behind home plate. They were great seats." Frankie smiled at Tony. "When the game was over we walked back to the cycle. Tony got on first so I put my leg over the gas tank, and sat down pushing him back."

Everyone howled with laughter. Except for April who was shocked.

"When we left Frankie did not wait in line behind the other cars. She raced between the cars like she was Evel Kenevel. We get to the end of the line, She was next to a pickup. She was at his side when he turned right. She guns the cycle shooting ahead of him. The pickup honked, and waved at her with one finger. So of course Frankie returned the gesture as I hung on tight."

The table laughed as April said "Oh my lord" She shook her finger at Frankie, "we're going to have to talk young lady."

As the evening wore on the family talked asking questions. The children were excited since their Uncle had gone into space, and was on the space station. Tony holding Frankie's hand walked to the back yard. As they stared at the moon Tony said "growing up with my brothers was hell. They constantly tormented me. I learned if I got mad yelling at them it was only worse. So I don't say anything, and don't give them a fight. Their teasing runs its course, and they don't get a fight, which is what they want." Frankie kissed him "Well I'm not going to stand for it. I will kick their butt if they don't behave.

Tony with his arm around her waist pulled her close, kissing her "it will do no good, they won't learn from it, and you will just be tired."

Chapter III

Frankie woke early. She looked around the room realizing she was in Oregon. She smiled thinking Tony was in his room across the hall. She thought about going into his room, and waking him with a kiss. She decided not to since April seemed to be sensitive about their relationship. She stretched thinking of Tony's family. They were nice. She frowned thinking of his two brothers. No wonder Tony referred to them as Bevis, and Butthead. She didn't like them. She did like the rest of the family. She kicked the covers off stepping out of bed. She made the bed then taking her clothes, and makeup, headed to the bathroom. She smiled as she thought of April. She thought about how she looked like a flower child from the seventies.

When she finished dressing she went down stairs to the kitchen. John smiled at her when she walked in.

"Good morning Frankie."

"Good Morning."

"Would you like some tea, honey."

"I would like some coffee if you have some."

April frowned as she reached for a cup filling it with coffee. She handed it to her, then filled John's cup.

"You know coffee has no nutritional value."

"It has caffeine, and caffeine is our friend." John said, smiling at April.

"Caffeine is not your friend." April said as she went to the oven taking out a glass dish.

"Are you from Houston?" John asked."

"No I'm from Tucson. My Dad, and Mom have a small, old truck stop where my Dad is a mechanic, and Mom runs the cafe that is next to it."

"Tucson, honey the desert sun is harsh on your skin." April said as she walked quickly out of the room. She returned, handing her a small tube. "This is aloe vera with some other natural ingredients. It will help keep your skin moisturized."

"I think she has beautiful skin.

"And we want to keep it that way, John."

Frankie giggled as John shrugged.

"Is your name Frankie, or is that a nickname?"

"My name is Francis, after my grandmother. My Dad's name is Frank, so I'm Frankie.

Tony walked in, and kissed Frankie on the cheek. He walked to the counter pouring himself a cup of coffee.

April frowned "Good morning Tony."

"Morning Mom."

He sat down as John sat his cup down.

Well I'm glad you decided not to sleep all day."

Tony sipped the strong coffee. "I didn't get much sleep last night. Frankie kept sneaking into my room."

John laughed.

"She did not, now stop acting like your Dad." April said, sitting down the casserole on the counter, going to the cupboard getting the plates.

"Well he did put up a pretty good fight." Frankie said smiling

"Don't encourage him." April said, sitting down.

They talked of Houston, and what was happening at NASA. Tony said there was talk of reinstating the shuttle. John said they would go to see Jase, and Jacolb who were Ricky's boys play baseball. They would stop, and pick up his Dad, and Mom who were in an assisted living center. Frankie offered to help clean up, but April politely refused saying she was a guest.

John stopped his pickup at an apartment complex. He went inside, and came out later followed by his parents. April stepped out of the front seat allowing John's Dad to sit in the front seat. Frankie slid over close to Tony. John helped his mother step into the pickup. She introduced herself, Crystal, and Joel. She liked to talk, and asked Frankie many questions.

They arrived at the park taking out their chairs. Sissy, and Dean were there as well as Bobby, and his wife, and children. Ricky was coach of the little league team. His son Josh played pitcher. His youngest son played second base. Frankie was surprised how patient Ricky was as a Coach. When the right fielder threw the ball into the infield, and the third baseman had to chase it, he patiently, and gently explained how the shortstop should have gone to the outfield, and the right fielder should always throw to the cut off man. He encouraged the kids, and when they lost the game he told them how great they played.

Crystal sat next to Frankie talking constantly. Her husband did not say much. Frankie played with the twin girls who were four. The family gathered together having hamburgers, and hotdogs. It was a pleasant afternoon. Ricky, and Bobby did not give Tony a hard time. The children all wanted to hear about going to space. Frankie enjoyed herself. April told her how Tony was not planned; she was forty one when he was born. Sissy would look after him when she was at the store. She told when she was going to school at Berkeley, she met John. He was a Green Beret scheduled to go to VietNam. She was at a protest rally when he started flirting with her.

Frankie laughed "you were protesting the VietNam war, and John was in the military?"

"Well I wasn't against the soldiers, I was against the government who had us in a senseless war.

Frankie laughed.

"We dated until he was deployed. I wrote to him while he was there, and when he returned we were married. My parents were shocked since they were against the war."

"They were hippies." Frank said as he watched the children play.

"They certainly were not. They were people who loved everyone, even soldiers. They were against the war. We raised our own food, and rarely ate meat."

"Hippies."

"Stop it John. Well anyway they are both with the Lord."

Frankie couldn't help but giggle.

Later that evening, arriving at home, they sat on the front porch talking enjoying the cool evening. When they went inside they walked up the stairs to the second floor. Tony kissed Frankie on the cheek as he went into his room Going into her room Frankie saw as April turned looking over her shoulder as she went in her room. Frankie changed into her shorts, and long tee shirt. She waited for a short time then carefully opened the door. She went on tiptoes to Tony's room, she opened the door slowly going inside. She went to his bed sitting down. She put her hand on his face leaning over kissing him.

"I thought I would tuck you in."

Tony kissed her, "You could join me."

Frankie smiled "Oh no, we're not ready for that step."

"I am."

"You were ready on our first date." She kissed him. "Good night Tony," then on her tiptoes went back to her bed.

The following morning Frankie walked into the kitchen wearing a nice conservative dress. It covered her shoulders, and went to her knees. April brought her a cup of coffee smiling at her. Frankie knew she had passed a test. She knew April with her critical eye approved. Tony wore a light blue polo with khaki pants with his stylish shoes. His short hair with the top spiked looked good. She kissed him on the cheek. "You sleep good last night?"

"No, I was thinking of a midnight prowler all night."

They drove through Salem to the big brick Methodist Church. The family all sat together. Joel, and Crystal came in with the other senior citizens. They had ridden the shuttle which drove them to church each Sunday. When the announcements were concluded Dean, and Sissy left with children following. They were in charge of the children's church. The service was much as Frankie had expected. When it ended many people who knew Tony since he had been raised in the church were anxious to talk to him. He introduced Frankie, and talked of what was happening at NASA. They left going to Sissy's house for dinner.

When dinner was over they told the family goodby. They drove to the log cabin where Tony, and Frankie prepared to leave. April cried as she hugged Frankie telling her to please write, and she was welcomed to come back. She hugged Tony then turned walking into the house. John drove them to the airport. He walked with them to the plane. As Tony went through the pre-flight checklist John talked with Frankie. He opened the door for her, and helped her in. She smiled knowing that was his nature. John watched as the plane taxied to the runway then began to pick up speed, it lifted off the ground, and headed Southeast. He sighed thinking "He's a good pilot.

Chapter IV

Tony maneuvered through traffic which moved steadily. He watched the traffic carefully since he was on a motorcycle. Vehicles often did not see the cycle so he always rode with caution. The Kawasaki 750 he rode glided down the highway effortlessly. He turned off the busy highway onto a two lane blacktop, then three miles turned on his street heading for his house. He smiled as he turned into his driveway seeing the black Jaguar sports car sitting in his driveway. He parked beside the Jaguar that belonged to Frankie. He stepped off the cycle removing his helmet as he walked to the door.

Walking inside he saw Frankie come out of the kitchen. She smiled broadly. "Welcome home honey." She hugged him kissing him as Tony put his arms around her pulling her closer

"This is a great welcome home, I could get used to this."

She smiled, kissing him then stepped back. Dinner is almost ready."

He walked to the bathroom washing his hands, and then went into the kitchen where Frankie sat a glass of ice tea on the table.

"It's organic."

Tony sipped the tea, "no its not, its lipton."

Frankie smiled, shrugging her shoulders. She removed a pan from the oven sitting it on the counter. Tony sat two plates with forks, and knives on the table.

"The lasagna needs to cool then we can eat." She sat a loaf of garlic bread on the table cutting a piece sitting it on his plate. "So honey, how was work?"

Tony bit into the bread which was good. He smiled being suspicious.

"Well, we are retrofitting the Atlantas. It was the last shuttle to the Space Station. We have a new Director, and congress is more friendly to NASA. The Russians are being stubborn with Americans flying on their rockets. It's been decided we should use our own shuttles. and the shuttle can carry a bigger payload."

"Why did we stop using the shuttle in the first place?"

"Money. It was expensive using the shuttle. NASA, well actually congress found it cheaper to use the Russian rockets to fly to the Space Station."

Frankie went to the counter bringing the lasaguana to the table. She cut a large piece for Tony then herself. She sat down bowing her head. Tony prayed then they began eating. Tony waited for Frankie to speak.

Finally Frankie said "Memorial day is coming, I'm off for the weekend. I thought it would be good to go home. Memorial day is a big deal for my family, they always get together."

Tony wiped his mouth

"So you're inviting me?"

She looked at Tony, "of course I am. I think it's time you met the wild bunch. I was thinking with your plane we could be in Tucson in a couple of hours."

"So when you say wild bunch, what exactly do you mean?"

Frankie looked at her lasagna, she cut a piece then looked at Tony.

"They're different from your family. They are, say, more assertive." She looked down then took a bite of lasagna.

"Assertive?"

She wiped her mouth, taking a drink of tea. "You know how your brothers give you a hard time. Well that's amature hour compared to my family." She hesitated as she looked at Tony. "You will need to be more assertive with them."

"You don't think I'm assertive?"

She sat back looking at him. "You are a great guy, intelligent, handsome, with a good personality, and I'm falling in love with you. But my family can be loud, argumentative, sometimes obnoxious, and they will run over you if you don't stand up for yourself."

She stood up walking to the sink. She looked back at Tony. "I just want you to know they are good christian people. My Mother is a strong willed woman. Perhaps too strong."

Tony walked to her, putting his arms around her waist.

"So you love me." She tried to pull back, but he pulled her closer. "I love you." He kissed her. She stepped back walking back to the table sitting down.

"My family is not a bunch of psychopaths, but sometimes they may act like it. They can be a rough bunch." She started to say more then decided not too. "You will like them, but please don't judge them until you get to know them. I want you to keep an open mind."

Tony sat down. "Okay."

They finished supper, and when the dishes were cleaned Tony walked Frankie to her car. "I would like to leave Friday when you get off work."

"OKay, I'll pick you up, and we will fly to Tucson."

Tony worked through the week on the shuttle. On Friday he asked his supervisor if he could leave at three. His supervisor frowned at him. "Why not, most took off the whole day. Sure go ahead, and leave at three."

Tony called Frankie telling her he would pick her up at four. Frankie called her Mother letting her know they would arrive at the Tucson airport about six thirty.

Frankie was waiting at the door when Tony arrived in his Ford Ranger. She smiled as she stepped out the door walking quickly to the pickup placing her suitcase in the back. Stepping in the pickup she saw Tony was wearing a teal colored polo shirt, denim painter pants, and leather high top tennis shoes. His short hair was neatly combed with the top spiked. She smiled thinking of the impression he would make on her family.

Jackie Daniels standing inside the airport watching as planes landed, and took off. She saw from the south a small Cessna plane slowly descend, touching down on the long runway. She watched as it taxied onto a seperate road leading to the hangars. She walked out of the airport towards the plane. Frankie stepped out of the plan walking towards her Mother. She embraced her as Jackie hugged her. She stepped back as Tony with the suitcases walked around the plane. She looked at Tony as Frankie said "Mom this is my friend Tony."

Jackie stared at the young man. Tony sat the bags down looking at the tall slender woman with dark hair, and brown eyes. She looked like Frankie only older. He smiled, extending his hand. Jackie shook his hand. "I'm Jackie."

Tony followed Frankie, and Jackie to the airport. He sat the luggage down, walked to an office to make arrangements for the plane.

Jackie said "He's not what I expected."

"What did you expect." Frankie's words were sharp.

Jackie turned looking at the daughter "Don't be rude, I just didn't expect him to be," she hesitated "so preppy."

"He's an engineer, also an astronaut. What do you think they would be like."

"Watch your tone with me Frankie!" She stepped closer, her hands on her hip.

Frankie did not back up, "He's really a nice guy, and I love him."

Jackie stepped back as Tony walked up. The tension was heavy in the air.

"We're all set."

Jackie smiled, walking off with Frankie, and Tony following.

Tony placed the luggage in the back of the Ford F one fifty. Frankie sat in the front seat. Shutting the door to the back seat he said "this looks like my Dad's pickup.

Jackie smiled as she drove out of the airport.

It was a quiet ride when Jackie broke the silence. "So Tony, Frankie says you're an astronaut."

"I'm an engineer who has gone through astronaut training. I did go to the International Space Station two years ago. It was a bit scary. Just imagine sitting in a rocket that was built by the lowest bidder."

Jackie laughed "government at its finest."

Frankie, and Jackie talked of Tucson, and the truck stop. Jackie slowed down pointing to her left. "That's the truckstop. Frank runs the gas station, and mechanic shop, while I run the cafe. We do a good business."

Tony could see out the tinted windows, what appeared to be an old fashioned gas station with pumps. A cafe connected to the station.

"It looks nice. It has a nostalgic look."

Jackie glanced back at Tony then turned her attention to the road. "That's exactly the look Frank was going for." She looked at Frankie who smiled.

Jackie stopped the pickup in front of a nice brick home. Tony was impressed with the modern look. The yard was a rock garden with cactus, and yucca plants. In the driveway were five motorcycles. Two men were standing beside them. The older man had long hair down to his shoulders, with a full beard. He was tall with broad shoulders, and long arms. The younger man was taller with a barrel chest, and powerful arms. He had a short haircut with a trimmed full beard.

They both walked to the pickup. The older man hugged Frankie, picking her up. "Girl its been too long since you've been home"

Frankie hugged the man tightly. She hugged the younger man then smiling broadly said "Daddy, Roger this is my friend Tony. Tony, this is my Dad Frank Daniels, and my brother Roger."

Frank stared at the young man in front of him. He was clean shaven short hair that was spiked on top. Wearing a polo shirt, and painter pants.

Tony extended his hand."It's a pleasure to meet you sir." Frank shook Tony's hand,nodding. Tony shook Rogers hand as he stared at him.

"Well let's go in the house," Jackie said, taking Frank's hand.

The door opened as a young woman ran out of the house, she threw her arms around Frankie.

"Oh girl I have missed you!"

Frankie laughed hugging her. She smiled broadly "Tony this is Jody, She's Roger's wife."

Jody looked at Tony then hugged him. With her arms around Tony's neck she looked over her shoulder at Frankie. "He's a hottie."

Tony's face turned red. "That's enough now Jody," Jackie said, trying not to laugh. "Let's not scare him off."

Jody put her small hand on Tony's face leaning close as her arm was around his neck. "Yes sir, you're some kind of pretty man."

Frankie stepped up taking Jody's hand "easy girl Tony's shy."

Jody stepped back laughing as the others snickered. Tony's face was red as he followed Jackie into the house.

Jackie led Frankie, and Tony through the house which was decorated in southwestern style. She opened a door saying "I've kept your room the same as you left it. She walked down the hall opening a door. "This is the office, I hope you don't mind sleeping on a cot."

"Tony smiled "not a problem."

Tony looked at the meal in front of them. Fried chicken, fried potatoes, fried squash, fried okra, everything was fried except for the ice tea. Frank prayed for the meal then the family began to fill their plates. Frankie watched as Tony placed a piece of chicken on his plate then okra, and potatoes.

"Meals are a little different here."Tony nodded as he ate.

"Tony what's your parents do for a living?" Frank asked, looking down the table at Tony.

"My dad's a contractor. He, and my two brothers are carpenters, electricians, HVAC, plumbers. They have a good business. My Mother is, well she has a herbal shop where she, and my sister work."

Frankie sat her fork down. "April, Tony's Mother has the most amazing greenhouses. She literally has every herb, and plant you can imagine. She not only grows plants, she also extracts oil, and makes her own products."

Jackie was impressed "she's into essential oils?"

"Actually April was into herbs, and oils before essential oils were popular. She is a believer in healthy living with supplements. She is amazing, she knows so much about health, and which products go together for whatever ailments a person has."

"That includes marijuana?" Roger who was a deputy sheriff for Tempe Arizona asked as he stared at Tony.

"Yes, she has one greenhouse of just marijuana. She has always believed in the medicinal value of marijuana. She doesn't approve of using it to get high."

Roger skoffed "people use it to get high. Now it's legal."

Tony looked passively at Roger. "Mom is a licensed grower. She uses the oil, but she does sell it to other shops who sell it for those who chose to smoke it."

Roger sneered at Tony. "Yeah right, just an excuse to get high. She's making money from selling drugs."

"Yeah, I guess she is like the pharmaceutical drug companies."

The tension was heavy as the two stared at each other.

"Of course you're right, marijuana has not always been legal. Oregon did pass medical, and recreational use of marijuana. Mom believing in its healing value raised it for years. She processed it, and sold the oil to customers who wanted healing, not just to get high. The local sheriff did not agree so he constantly raided her green houses. I remember when I was five, I was sitting in the living room watching cartoons, eating cereal. When there was a loud knock on the door. It flew open, and men in black with helmets on, their face covered, all had a high powered rifle. Screaming "get down!" So I sat my bowl of cereal down, and laid down. My Mom, and sister came out of the kitchen, they were making cupcakes. Men pointing guns in their face screaming so they laid down. The DEA, and Sheriff's office searched the house, and greenhouses including the entire grounds. They handcuffed my Mom taking her to the Sheriff's office. Even though they didn't find anything. She said they screamed, and yelled at her for two hours. They threatened her with prison. When Dad showed up it took the entire force to restrain him, and put him in jail. His lawyer showed up, and they released Mom, but were afraid to release Dad. They finally did, and there were no charges. When they would raid the house the Sheriff's office would always go by the job where he was working to tell him they had a warrant to search the premises. He would come home, they would search the place and never find anything."

The room was quiet as they looked at Tony.

Jody snickered "I can imagine a five year old child eating his froot loops, and SWAT shows up."

"Cherro's Mom didn't allow sugar."

Roger sat shaking his head "it's against the law. Whether you agree, or not, it's the law."

Tony began eating as the family sat quietly eating their meal.

"Did you work in the family business growing up?" Frank asked, breaking the tension.

"I hauled chicken poop for Mom's all natural plants. I would do odd's, and end's jobs for Dad. He makes his money from big jobs. If a sink, or bathtub needed replaced, a hot water heater replaced, or a garbage disposal needs installed, or fixed he would send me. He would say "boy i'm glad you don't work for the fire department. As slow as you are, half the city would burn down.""

Jackie laughed looking at Roger "sound familiar."

Roger smiled.

When supper was finished, and the dishes cleared the family moved to the living room with the large wooden leather furniture. Frankie, and Tony sat on the settee. The family talked of what was happening in their lives.Tony talked of growing up in Oregon, attending school at Stanford then getting his masters at Oklahoma then his Phd at Texas.

"Why Oklahoma?" Jody asked.

I was stationed at Tinker. They have AWacks which I was trained on, Norman was not far, so I went to OU before I was deployed.

Roger looked at Tony "You served in the military?"

"Air Force."

"Air Force!" Roger said, sneering at Tony.

"My Dad was a Green Beret in VietNam, My brothers were Airborne Rangers in Afghanistan, and Iraq. I wanted to fly so I joined the Air Force."

"Must have been tough flying around safe from the action."

"It was a good assignment, there was a time we hit some hard turbulence, I spilled coffee on my hand burning it."

The family giggled. Frankie put her arm around Tony. "Oh my poor baby, you burned yourself."

"I found a first aid kit, and put some salve on it, and wrapped it in some gauze."

"That's my man struggling through adversity." Frankie kissed him on the cheek.

Frank was smiling "when did your Dad serve in VietNam?"

"1970 to 1971."

"I was there 1969 to 1970." He sat quietly for a while then said "Wasn't pleasant over there. I imagine Afghanistan, and Iraq wasn't a picnic." He looked at Roger "I respect all who serve, whether in the air, sea, or ground."

The talk soon turned to the ride they would make tomorrow. Frankie casually said to Tony "we ride every year on Memorial Day. We will be going to the Grand Canyon where other clubs will gather, it's fun you'll like it. Dad has an extra bike for you to ride."

Tony sat quiet as he heard Roger say "you do know how to ride?"

"Sure I ride my bike to work everyday."

Roger looked surprised "what kind of bike do you ride?"

"A Kawasaki 750."

Roger put his head back laughing "a rice burner!"

Frankie leaned forward "Tony's 750 would smoke your hog any day"

"I doubt that."

They stared at each other when Frank said "I think Tony will be fine."

Chapter V

Tony opened his eyes when he felt the cot shaking. Frank was looking down at him.

"Wake up, today we ride."

Tony pushed the covers off him, dressed, and went to the bathroom with his shaving bag. When he walked into the dining room the table was set with breakfast. He sat down as Frankie brought him a cup of coffee. Roger looked at him disapprovingly. Tony was wearing a blue tee shirt with painter pants, and tennis shoes. The others were wearing black Harley Davidson tee shirts. He just didn't fit in.

As the family ate they talked of the ride. Frank explained they would meet the Tombstone chapter then pick others up as they traveled. Frankie said her family was a christian chapter. Other chapters would be joining them.

"He's not flying our colors." Roger said sharply looking at Frankie.

Frankie's eyes narrowed as her anger began to flare.

"No, because he's not in the chapter, jackass."

Roger sat his fork down. "Watch your mouth little girl."

"Or what, you're going to give me that cop attitude!"

"What the hell is that supposed to mean!"

"You have a high opinion of yourself!"

"You're about to push it too far Frankie!"

Frankie was standing up fist clenched, "you need to show more respect, or I'll kick your ass!"

"You going to fight his battles, can't your pretty boy fight for himself!"

"I'd enjoy doing it myself, I don't want Tony to get dirty!"

Roger was on his feet "Well let's see what you got, I think your all mouth!"

Jackie was on her feet "Both of you sit down! I won't have this kind of talk at my table!"

She stared hard at Roger, and Frankie. "You'll sit down, or I will have your Father do it for you." They both stared at her. "Frank!"

When he stood up both sat down.

"Tony is a guest in this house, and you will show him respect"

"Sure why not!"

"Careful how you speak to your Mother!"

Roger raised his hands "I'm sorry."

Frank looked directly at Frankie pointing his finger "you watch that temper!"

Frankie nodded.

Frank, and Jackie sat down. "I apologize for that Tony."

"It's ok."

Frankie stood up walking away. The rest sat quietly eating. When she returned sitting next to Tony. She held up a jean jacket with the sleeves out.

"Tony has his own colors. If you would not have been so." she glanced at her Mother "obnoxious I would have shown you."

Tony looked at the worn sleeveless jacket. It had a NASA patch on the front. On the back was a NASA logo, a space helmet in the center, with the name Sky Walker on the bottom. He smiled as Frankie said "may the force be with you."

Frankie brought a sleeping bag to Tony's room. She showed him how to roll up his clothes in the sleeping bag. She told him to leave his shaving kit. He wouldn't need it, only his toothbrush, and toothpaste. They would travel light taking only the necessities. She was wearing a jean jacket with patches on.

"I have a friend who works in housekeeping. Actually we go to church with her. Anyway she found this jean jacket in a second hand store. When I came to see you at NASA, I stopped at the gift store, and purchased the patches. Tammy found the helmet design online, and she did the embroidery."

She explained how each club had their own name, and patches. They were not any different than other clubs. Colors were the name of the club. Only members were allowed to wear or fly their colors."

Tony followed her outside where she strapped the sleeping bag on with bungee cords. The motorcycle he was riding had saddlebags like the others. Frankie explained the food, and cooking utensils, all would share in carrying them in the saddlebags. Frank explained the bike which was similar to his Kawasaki. The gears were one down, and four up. He would have to get used to the clutch since they were all different. Frankie handed a helmet, and a pair of goggles to Tony.

He frowned. "It doesn't have a face shield."

Frankie put on her helmet "adjust sweetheart."

Frank, and Roger did not wear helmets. Jackie, Frankie, Jody, and Tony did. Frank, and Jackie led the group as Roger with Jody on the back pulled out. The motorcycle died as Tony released the clutch. He started it then pulled out as Frankie looked back. He rode beside her as they traveled through Tucson.

On the north edge of the city a group of bikers sat waiting at a truck stop. They fell in behind as the group headed north on highway seventy-seven. Tony saw as they were out of the city Frank, Jackie, Roger, and Frankie all sat back on the bike placing their feet on the pegs on the front of the bike. He was nervous, but he leaned back resting his feet on the front pegs. It was comfortable. He was concerned as the group picked up speed. He glanced at the speedometer which was showing seventy five. He was not used to traveling at such speed. He glanced at Frankie who seemed at ease, and looked natural riding the big Harley Davidson. He tried to relax as the country seemed to fly past him. Jody wearing a black scarf covering her nose, and mouth turned looking at Tony. She winked at him then turned around.

They traveled for over two hours. When they reached Holbrook where they turned west on I forty. A large group of bikers joined them as they headed west. They stopped at Flagstaff where a large group of bikers were parked at a large truck stop. Frank pulled in as the rest followed. All of the bikers lined up to fill up. Tony had never seen so many bikers. He put the kickstand down standing up stretching. Frankie beside him smiled broadly, "How do you like the ride so far?

Tony removed his helmet. "We're making good time."

"Dad likes to get down the road."

Frankie knew most of the people, and they all wanted to talk with her. She introduced Tony as her friend. They all looked at his jean jacket. They were all wearing a jacket. Each of them with different patches, and different names representing their chapter. They were all christian bikers.

Frank, and Jackie knew all the bikers. They talked for a while resting from the ride. They went inside which was filled with bikers. Many of them talked with Frankie. They sat at a long table with a group of bikers. Tony ordered a Club sandwich, the others all ordered hamburgers, and fries . He sat quietly as the group talked. Many of them asked questions of Tony who had been in space. He couldn't help, but notice how the young men talked with Frankie. With lunch finished the bikers headed north for the grand canyon.

When they arrived there were a large number of bikes at the grand canyon campgrounds. Frank stopped at an open area. The group stepped off their bikes. The campsite was set up. Frankie taking off her sleeping bag said "It will be a nice night so we will sleep under the stars." Tony took off the sleeping bag from the back of the bike, and unrolled it close to Frankies.

He smiled "you know they can be one big sleeping bag."

Frankie smiled "Oh no sweetheart, my Dad is just starting to like you. He would feel bad beating you to death."

It was a warm day as the bikers sat, or enjoyed walking around looking at the bikes, and talking to people they had not seen for a while. A large fire was built, and the chapter from Tucson sat eating sandwiches. It was late in the evening when Jody smiled "I think you may have gotten a little too much sun Tony."

"I believe I did."

Roger grunted "not much sun inside your air conditioned office."

"Don't pay any attention to him Tony, Roger's been cranky for a long time."

"I'm not cranky!

"No, you would rather be with your boys than here."

"You're crazy, what are you talking about?"

Jody stood up "You work with your buddies all day at the Sheriff's office, then every weekend you ride with them. Leaving me, and Cody at home."

"I have a tough job, and like to unwind! You don't have any idea what I'm going through!"

Jody was now furious "What about me? You don't think of anyone, but yourself. It's always about you!

Roger was mad as he stood up "I take care of you, and Cody!"

"You're never home, and when you are you complain about the scum you have to deal with. I take Cody to his games which you don't bother to come to!"

The group sat quietly as the argument escalated.

"You just want someone to take care of your child, cook, and clean for you. I'm not your maid, and occasional play thing!"

She was on the verge of tears. When Roger shouted "I'll buy you a bike so you can ride anytime you want to!"

"I don't want to ride a bike, I'm not Jackie, or Frankie! I love to ride behind you. I suppose we all know what that is, the bitch seat! I guess that makes me a." She stopped speaking as she turned walking off crying when Jackie was on her feet. She walked to Jody grabbing her by the arm spinning her around. Jody looked up at Jackie who grabbed her hugging her. She held her tight to her body.

"You will never use that vulgar term again. I love you, and don't care if you ride your own bike. I don't want you to be like me, or Frankie. I love you for being you."

Both women held onto each other as Jody cried. Jackie stepped back, taking Jody by the hand. She walked back to the campfire where Roger stood. She looked at Frank "I want you to beat some sense into your son."

Frank stood walking towards Roger. Roger stepped back "Hold on, I'm sorry." Frank looked hard at Roger as he stepped towards his son.

As the tension grew Tony said "It won't do any good you'll just get tired."

Frank, and Roger both looked at him. Tony stood up "He's too hard headed, and it's not right for you to whip him. I'll do it."

They looked at him surprised. Frankie burst out laughing. Then Jackie, and Jody laughed. Frank stepped back laughing "Ok killer he's all yours!" Roger looked at the smaller man then laughed.

He walked to Jody taking her hand "I'm sorry, you're right, I haven't spent enough time with you. I promise next weekend me, and you will ride together." He hugged her. They walked back to the fire sitting down.

Tony said "does this mean I don't get to whip him?"

Frank held up his hands "No, please, we don't need any violence. Just calm down killer."

The group laughed as Frankie stood up putting her arm around Tony.

"Easy there big boy, calm down."

Tony, and Frankie sat down as the rest of the group around the campfire laughed.

Tony removed his shoes, and socks. He crawled into the sleeping bag, and looked at Frankie who was in her sleeping bag next to him. She smiled at him.

"You did a good job breaking the tension."

"I know, I could have killed him. That would probably have made a bad impression on your parents."

Frankie giggled. "Good night Tony."

Chapter VI

Tony woke up when he felt someone kicking his feet. He looked up, seeing Frank looking down at him.

"You normally sleep all day?"

Tony sat up rubbing the sleep out of his eyes. He saw the rest of the group sitting at the fire looking at him.

"Sorry, I thought for a minute there I was back in Oregon, and my Dad was kicking my feet wanting me to go to work. It must have been a flashback."

The people all laughed as Tony got out of the sleeping bag, and walked in his bare feet to the fire. Jackie handed him a cup of coffee. Tony sipped the strong black coffee.

"Wow that's an eye opener."

"It's campfire coffee, haven't you ever had strong coffee?" Frank asked, smiling.

"Well no, not this strong. In the boy scouts we usually didn't make it so strong."

"You were a boy scout?" Frankie asked.

"Yes, actually an eagle scout. Dad was the scout master so he pushed me, Bevis, and Butthead until we made eagle scout."

"Okay, now I'm impressed, an eagle scout." Frankie said as she put her arms around Tony.

"When Ricky, and Bobby joined the scouts Dad was assistant scoutmaster. He later became the scoutmaster. When I graduated people thought he would quit, but he stayed for another five years."

"Your Dad is a good man," Frank said looking at Tony.

Tony finished his coffee, picking up his clothes, and headed for the washroom.

When he came back he had breakfast, which was a simple bowl of oatmeal. Jody sitting next to him put her arm around him, her head on his shoulder.

"You smell good!"

Roger looked at Jody from across the table, "Ya know I took a shower."

"I know you always use old spice.

"I thought you liked it?"

"I do, but it may be time for change."

She sat up removing her arm holding her hand up at Roger.

"Easy there big boy, let's not rile him up! We don't need any trouble."

The group at the table snickered.

"Don't make me come over there, and give you a stern lecture. You wouldn't want that;"

Tony said as he finished his oatmeal."

The Tucson chapter walked together where church services were conducted. A group of teenagers led the singing. With a keyboard, and guitar they sang traditional hymns, and more modern praise songs. The Tucson chapter sang loud, and clapped their hands Tony smiled thinking his church was more subdued. He loved their singing.

It was a good service as the preacher with a long beard, and hair to his shoulders led the service. Frank, and Jackie shouted Amen, Praise God, as did others in the chapter. The service ended, with a long prayer, Jackie with her head bowed began speaking in a language Tony did not understand. He had never heard anyone speak in tongues.

When it was over they gathered for lunch of hotdogs.

Jackie asked. "did you enjoy the service Tony?"

"I did, The service was good, I enjoyed the music. My church is somewhat more subdued."

"We're a little more enthusiastic." Frankie said, looking at Tony.

He stood up carrying his plate to the garbage can.

"No reason to be judgemental."

"I wasn't being judgemental!"

"You were, and sarcastic."

She stood up walking to the garbage can "I was not sarcastic, I was making a true statement."

"Ok, well I'm glad you set me straight, I misunderstood, I apologize for my ignorance."

Frankie felt anger as she stared at Tony who passively looked back at her.

He turned around walking off. She started to follow him when she felt a strong hand on her arm. She looked at her Dad.

"Might be best to let him go. You shouldn't talk with him while you're angry."

Frankie walked away knowing her Dad was right.

A large group of motorcycles roared out of the campsite riding around the canyon. It was spectacular seeing the beauty of the canyon as well as the landscape. They rode to the north side of the canyon where they stopped at an overlook area.

After the ride they returned sitting around talking. Frankie sitting next to Tony said quietly "I didn't mean to sound critical earlier today."

"Yes you did, my Mother insulted you, and you still carry the anger of her being judgemental."

Frankie sat looking at Tony. She was surprised, and angry.

"I'm trying to apologize, and you won't accept it. Don't the Methodist forgive?"

Tony stood up walking away.

That evening they attended another service then went back to their camp. Frankie holding Tony's hand walked away from the group.

"I am sorry," she said softly.

Tony held both her hands. I"m sorry also. I suppose I am sensitive about my family, and religion. I'm not like you. I don't express myself the same as you. I'm sorry.?"

She kissed him, and walked back to the camp. They headed out the following day.

It was impressive as the bikers all left the campsite. Hundreds of Harley Davidson motorcycles roared out of the park early in the morning. Some of the bikers riding single while others riding on the back. It was a good ride as bikers turned east at Flagstaff. Roger, and Jody continued south for Phoenix. As the bikers turned south on Highway seventy-seven many bikers continued east. They arrived in Tucson by three in the afternoon.

The motorcycles were parked, and unloaded. Jackie, and Frankie began preparing supper.

Jackie asked Tony "you did say you worked on garbage disposal?'

"Yes, I have."

"My garbage disposal is down at the cafe. Would you mind looking at it?"

"I wouldn't mind at all."

Frank drove to the small truck stop. He stopped at the back of the cafe. Tony followed Frank to his garage where he picked up a set of allen wrenches. Frank said as he walked.

"Rosie runs the cafe when Jackie isn't there. She can be cantankerous at times. Keep in mind it's her kitchen."

Tony followed Frank into the kitchen. He saw a large woman at the grill. She had dark hair with streaks of gray. She scowled at them.

Frank said "Tony is here to fix the garbage disposal."

Rosie nodded her head, and looked back to her grill.

Tony went to the sink looking under it seeing the garbage disposal. He turned on the switch, it made no sound. Frank said "I had a guy look at it, he said it needed replacing."

Tony looked at the bottom of the disposal.

"The disposal has a switch that is thrown if the motor gets too hot."

He pushed the red button under the motor. He turned on the switch, and it began humming. He turned off the switch. He took out an allen wrench inserting it in the small opening at the bottom of the disposal unit. It was too small. He tried several more until he found the one that fit.

"A long rod runs to the motor which turns the plate that has two chopping heads attached. This allen wrench should turn the rod." Tony tried to turn the wrench without success. "I imagine your plumber is a distributor of garbage disposals. That's why he wanted to sell you a new one." He replaced the allen wrench, and stood up. "Do you have a broom?" Rosie pointed to the back of the room. A small mexican woman walked to the door opening it. Tony took out a broom, and a mop. He placed both of the wooden handles in the drain. "Hold on to the disposal so it doesn't move." Frank grasped the disposal unit as Tony began pushing with the broom, and mop. He pushed hard, then the plate moved. He removed the broom, and mop and turned the unit on. It began spinning.

Frank grinned "now that's a trick.

Rosie walked to Tony hugging him tightly. "Thank you honey, it has been a pain in the neck not having the garbage disposal." She looked at him saying "Is there anything I can do for you?"

"Hold on Rosie, that's Frankie's friend."

She grinned "Ok since it's Frankie friend." She kissed him on the cheek.

Tony's face was red. He looked at the small mexican woman. "Could you bring me a glass of ice cubes?"

She looked at him curiously walking off. When she returned Tony dumped the ice in the sink drain. He turned on the garbage disposal. "You should dump ice in the drain occasionally to sharpen the blades."

He put the broom, and mop in the closet, nodded to Rosie who winked at him. Frank, and Tony left.

Frankie, and Jackie preparing dinner talked about her, and Tony. Jackie asked "what is Tony's family like?"

"John is a lot like Dad actually, his two brothers constantly tease him which is just bullying. His sister is nice. April is," she hesitated, smiling. "Imagine what it was like in the early seventies. You remember the song Aquarius?"

Jackie nodded looking confused.

Frankie began swaying with her arms in the air, and singing "this is the dawning of the age of aquarius." she stopped singing. "That's April she's a flower child of the seventies."

Jackie laughed "you're kidding."

"No I'm not. Long blond hair with a ponytail, round John Lennon glasses, long floral print skirt, and sandals."

Jackie laughed.

"She is so smart, yet naive in some ways. She's afraid of heights, flying, and the government."

"I can't wait to meet her. I mean if, well you, and Tony seem to be getting along well."

Frankie smiled "he's different isn't he. Tony reminds me of his Mother. I really like him, I mean I love him."

Jackie patted her on the shoulder "you should hang on to him."

Frank, and Tony returned as supper was finished. Jackie was happy with the garbage disposal being repaired. Frank said grinning "I now know how to fix it when it goes down. We won't have to buy a new one for a while."

Frank, and Jackie drove Tony, and Frankie to the airport. They watched as it taxied down the runway picking up speed then lifting off.

"You think we will have an astronaut in the family?"

Frank holding Jackie's hand walking to the pickup. "I have no doubt."

Chapter VII

It was a pleasant summer. The gulf coast was humid, but with the wind blowing off the ocean brought relief. Tony, and Frankie spent time on the ocean deep sea fishing. Frankie usually caught the biggest fish. They grilled on weekends, attended baseball games, movies, and plays the city hosted. They enjoyed being together. Their relationship continued to grow. Alone in Frankie, or Tony's house the passion would often get intense. Frankie would always stop it getting up walking away from Tony.

"I'm sorry, but I think we should wait."

She said one evening the passion they both felt had taken them to a point where the intemincy almost went too far. Frankie breathing hard stepped outside of Tony's house onto the deck looking at the ocean. She closed her eyes thinking how she wanted to be with him. She wanted to give herself to the man she loved. But she wanted to not take that step knowing it would change their relationship. She was not sure she wanted to go there. Tony stepped outside, he was frustrated. He loved Frankie, and knew she loved him. He wanted the relationship to go further.

"What's wrong?" He asked quietly.

"I love you, but I don't want to take our relationship to that level."

"Why not? I love you, and want to be with you."

She turned looking at him. "I love you Tony, but I don't want to have sex."

She walked away going to her car driving home. She had to get away knowing if she didn't she would sleep with Tony. She was confused. She wanted him, but also wanted to wait.

The following Sunday Tony walked into the Sunday School class. He looked good in his white polo, and blue slacks. He smiled sitting next to her. He leaned over whispering "I'm sorry I took things so far last night.

"It wasn't just you. I want to be with you, but feel we should wait."

He held her hand throughout the class, and service. He took her out for lunch then followed her home where they spent the day together. They attended evening service. When it ended he kissed her on the cheek. She watched him walk to his pickup, and drive off.

August was a hot month, and as the days went by meteorologists were forecasting a major hurricane heading into the Gulf of Mexico. Houston was in the path of hurricane Harvey. As the hurricane in the ocean built with intensity it headed for the coast. Tony drove his motorcycle to Frankie's house which was further north. She drove him to his house, and both began loading his pickup with his belongings. His neighbor across the street watched from his yard. With the last of the things Tony could load in his pickup, and Frankies car, He walked to his neighbor asking if he needed any help loading up to evacuate. The older man smiled as he looked at his neighbors who were loading their cars, and pickups.

"I've lived here for thirty years, and seen many hurricanes come, and go, me, and the wife will stay, and ride this one out."

A man who lived next to Tony came over. Listening to the man he said "this is not a typical hurricane it will be a major storm. The wind with the rain, and the surge from the ocean it will flood this neighborhood. I will help you gather your belongings so you can go."

"The man smiled, and nodded as his wife walked out. "We're going to be ok. I'll see you when you come crawling back."

Tony looked in disbelief "The city has ordered a mandatory evacuation."

"Seen 'em before. Me, and my wife will ride it out, same as before."

The man looked at Tony then to the man, and woman. "Mam if your husband is determined to stay I can take you with me to a safer place."

She smiled "we'll be ok, we have seen storms in the past."

"Good luck, and God be with you both." Tony said as he turned and walked away.

The man followed Tony, holding out his hand saying I'm Jimmy Smith, your neighbor."

"Tony Pierce, you heading north."

"Pecos, my wifes sister lives there."

Me, and my friend Frankie will be heading to San Antonio. She has a hotel room for us. We will be sleeping in separate beds."

JImmy laughed "good luck Tony I hope to see you when this is over. I fear our stubborn neighbor is in for a tough time."

"Good luck Jimmy."

They drove off with the neighborhood following them.

The traffic out of Houston was heavy. They made it to San Antonio checking into a hotel room with double beds. Each of them called family letting them know they were safe. Frankie's Reserve Unit was activated, and was to report the following day for search, and rescue. That night as Frankie, and Tony watched hurricane Harvey hit the coast of Texas, and Louisiana they felt the shock, and fear.

The storm hit San Antonio with a vengeance. Both wore shorts, and tee shirts to sleep in. Tony kissed Frankie lightly on the lips. He did not hold her, and she did not hug him. They looked at each other for a while then turned into their separate beds. They looked at each other in their separate beds as the storm raged.

"Now I know what it means so close yet so far away."

"Yeah," Frankie said softly as she looked at Tony who was only a few feet away.

FRANKIE WAS UP EARLY, she dressed in her uniform pinning on her rank of Major.

Tony watched Television seeing the devastation of the storm. He saw Frankie packing extra clothes preparing for a long duty. He kissed her holding her tight.

"Keep your feet dry."

"I'll try."

He watched her walk out the door.

Frankie arrived at the armory where trucks were being loaded with supplies. Boats attached to jeeps, and pickups were loaded with supplies. They left ahead of the rest. The men, and women who were veterans sat quietly as they made their way to Houston. Many of them had been deployed to New Orleans during hurricane Kartina. Remembering the scene in Louisiana, they all were aware of what Houston, and the communities surrounding it would be like. Some of the boats headed east while others headed west. The path of the hurricane was awesome. The Marines with the army, and sheriff's office along with the emergency management team had coordinated the rescue efforts prior to the hurricane. So when it hit the teams were sent out as soon as possible.

Rain was falling as the team placed their boat in the water. They slowly made their way seeing only the tops of roofs. People were found huddling together on the tops of roofs. People of all ages were brought into the boat. Frankie saw as other boats were helping people into their boats. She knew they were civilians who had come out to help. Sergeant Jefferies picked up a kitten who was swimming as the loaded boat headed for dry land. When they arrived, the tents were set up to feed, and help the injured. The look of shock apparent on peoples faces. They were helped out of the boats as people came to take them to the tents. The boat went back out into the deep water. As they traveled the boat would stop a civilian boat loaded with people, and animals. Frankie asked where they had been, not wanting to overlap. She would give them instructions where they should go, and always tell them thank you.

Frankie pointing said "starboard" The sergeant turned looking at where Frankie was pointing.

"By the tree."

He slowed as they approached a body floating face down. The crew pulled the body in the boat. Frankie checked the young man then placed a sheet over him.

The boat continued when she heard an emotional voice

"There on the roof."

Frankie's heart sank seeing a small body. She prayed it would be a doll. The boat turned, as it was close to the roof. Frankie stepped out carefully walking on the slick shingles. The water line was almost covering the roof. She bent down picking up the small child. She fought her emotions as she looked at the child. She walked back to the boat. Sergeant Jeffries with a strong hand gripped her arm as she stepped in. She placed the child under the sheet with the young man.

They slowly made their way through the underwater city. They picked up a dog, and a family of three. They made their way back in silence. Frankie checked out the family who were not injured. It was a long day, and when the team sat eating a Lieutenant Colonel walked in sitting next to Frankie.

"Major Daniels, I need your assistance in the medical tent."

"Yes Mam."

She followed her to a tent where many people were sitting outside. It was a sad sight seeing so many hurt, and suffering people.

Tony put on brown overalls, and work boots, he left San Antonio heading south. He could see where the Texas Department of

Transportation was clearing the roads. He knew as he drove through the trees that had been removed from the road men, and women with chainsaws were helping the state. He stopped at Frankie's house, the street was cluttered with tree branches. He saw the northwest side of the roof had lost a piece of decking. Most of the shingles were gone. The windows on the south side were broken. Going into the garage he found the tarps he had purchased early. Carrying one of them he crawled onto the roof covering the hole with the tarp. He cut up the piece of decking that had blown off, and used it to nail over the broken windows. He put his chain saw, and gas can in the pickup, and headed south.

He stopped seeing a large tent with men in uniform. He walked up to the tent, stopped, and waited as a Captain, and a man in a county sheriff's uniform talked. When he finished he walked up to the Captain.

"I have a chain saw, and gas, where do you want me to work?"

The Captain looked at him, "do you know how to sharpen a chainsaw blade?"

"Yes sir."

The Captain turned "Lieutenant, take this gentleman to Captain Goforth."

The Lieutenant immediately walked to a jeep with Tony following. The Lieutenant, a young man, said "we have a lot of chainsaw's clearing fallen trees. No one knows how to sharpen a blade when it gets dull."

Tony nodded his head as he saw the devastation. The jeep stopped at a sight where the sound of chainsaws running. Tony followed the Lieutenant to a man talking to three men holding chainsaws. He turned looking at them.

The lieutenant slauted "Captain Goforth this man," he looked at Tony "I didn't get your name sir."

"Tony Pierce."

"Mr. PIerce can sharpen chainsaw blades."

The Captain looked up smiling "Thank you Lord!" "Follow me Mr. Pierce."

Tony followed the Captain to a small tent where he saw several chainsaws sitting. He sat his chainsaw down. "You can use mine." He pulled a long slender file from his pocket on his leg and walked to the chainsaws.

The Captain said "Corporal Jenkins take this chainsaw, and see if you can clear this area."

The young Corporal grinned "Yes Sir." He picked up the chainsaw as Tony pointed to the gas can. He nodded picking it up, and left.

Holding the long skinny file in his right hand, and pushing gently with his left hand he began to sharpen the blade. Finishing the blade he started on the other when he heard the Captain say "Mr. Pierce." Tony looked up. "This is Privated Walters, and Private Gomez, would you show them how to sharpen a chainsaw blade?"

Tony nodded seeing two young girls wearing uniforms in front of him. They walked to him as he showed them how to hold the file. They watched carefully as he sharpened each blade. "See how dull it is?"

They both nodded watching him closely. He filed the blade moving slowly, "now it shines, it's sharp." he continued until he finished. He removed two files from his pocket handing one each to the young women. They began to sharpen blades as Tony watched. "You don't have to hit it too hard, just touch it up." The girls who were probably eighteen, learned quickly.

As they worked throughout the day chainsaws were brought to them with dull blades. Captain Goforth approached Tony "Sir I'm going to move the two Privates to assist in other areas. Would it be ok if they take the files with them"

"Absolutely."

"Thank you, I've notified headquarters to send files, and will make sure you get yours back."

"I'm not worried about that Captain."

Tony worked on chainsaws that stopped running, and put the blade on several that had come off. Each time he would reach into his pocket taking out a tool he needed.

He worked through the morning. When he had no other chainsaws he walked to the big tent where they were serving dinner. He washed his hands, and went inside where stew, and biscuits were served. He sat down in the crowded tent. The men, and women were tired.

A young man asked "are you a lumberjack sir. You seem to know chainsaws?"

"No, growing up in Oregon we cut a lot of firewood. I learned how to work on them from my Dad"

"Oh, so what do you do?"

"I'm an engineer at NASA, but today I'm a lumberjack."

The young men, and women at the table laughed. They asked questions about NASA, and going into space. When they finished they all headed back to work.

It had finally stopped raining, and the humidity with the sun was hot. As they worked A man arrived in a pickup, Tony sitting under a tree drinking water watched as he began to unload chainsaws. He stood up going to the deputy sheriff.

"I would appreciate it if you could get these going again, and the blades on some are dull."

Tony pulled the cord on one listening to it. He reached into his pocket taking out his multi tool, and removed the cover.

Captain Goforth watching him said "no sir, I believe your name is MacGyver. You seem to have everything you need."

"I was a boy scout, the motto was be prepared."

The captain laughed as he walked off.

Tony was able to get most of the chainsaws running. He told the deputy the parts he would need to repair the others. He worked until eight in the evening. He was tired as he ate his supper late in the evening. He rode with the Texas National Guard to where his pickup was parked. Exhausted he drove to Frankie's house. He used a bottle of water to clean himself since the water, and electricity was not on. He sent Frankie a Text.

U ok?

Yes, hell here.

House is ok?

Good U ok?

Yes, working with Tex Nat G. repairing Chainsaws.

You need to rest, can't get to Ur house, underwater.

Ok, get some rest. I love U

What's not to Love!

Nut. keep Ur feet dry.

I love U!

Tony talked to his Dad, then called Frank letting him know both were ok. Frank said the same thing as did his Dad "when you need me, call."

Chapter VIII

THE LONG HOURS WERE exhausting for Frankie who worked in the medical tent, then helped with logistics. She was released to go back to work at the hospital.

Tony worked with the Texas National Guard for four days. Other men, and women showed up helping him with the chainsaws. He told Captain Goforth, and the soldiers he was heading for his house which was near the coast. They thanked him, and told him they appreciated his help.

Felling apprehension Tony drove through the city seeing the devastation. It was like a war zone. Up rooted trees on houses, tree branches, and debris everywhere. He could see many people were starting the clean up process. He drove slowly down his street which still had mud on it. He stopped in front of his house stepping out of his pickup, shocked at his house. Mud was everwhery the house had obviously been covered in water. He took a deep breath as he looked at the house. Jimmy walked across his yard. He shook Tony's hand "glad to see you made it through."

"Yeah, San Antonio was hit hard, but this," He stopped as he stared in disbelief.

A woman walked up "I'm Nitta."

Tony shook her hand "Tony Pierce,"

Tony turned looking across the street at his neighbor's house which had a tree across the roof. "How did the neighbors fair?

"He, and his wife didn't make it. The Sheriff's office found him, and his wife two days ago."

They stood silently then Tony turned around, "I guess I should get to work."

"The city was by, and said to drag everything to the road, and when they get a chance they will pick it up." Jimmy said as he walked with Tony.

"Tony what about the pretty young girl in the sporty Jag?" Nita asked smiling

"She, and I spent the night in San Antonio in a hotel. It was hell."

"The storm was bad there?"

"Yes, but the tough part was sleeping in the same room with Frankie the most beautiful woman in the world in a separate bed."

Nitta giggled holding up her left hand pointing to her wedding band.

"You have work to do Nitta." Tony said as he walked to his pickup.

Using his cell phone Tony took pictures of his house. He cleared the mud from the front door, and walking inside began taking pictures of the devastation. He began scooping the mud out of his house. He stopped at noon, and called his Dad.

John listened as Tony described the damage. He was going to gut the house, and basically rebuild. When he hung up April sitting at the table listening without speaking, she looked up at John who had walked to the window looking out. He turned around "start packing, we're going to Houston."

April stood up walking to the stairs heading for the bedroom.

John loaded his trailer with supplies he thought he might need. Lumber, electrical wire, plumbing supplies, and his tools. April placed the wooden box with herbs, and oils in the back of the pickup. She placed the suitcase in the back seat then stepped into the passenger side. John started the pickup.

"Send a text to Tony, we should be there in three days."

April's fingers flew across the phone. Then sat back "Ricky, and Bobby upset they couldn't go?"

"Yeah, I told them to stay, and keep working. They wanted to come along, and help. Sissy cried when I told her to stay, and run the shop."

Frank pulled out of his house heading east with a trailer loaded with shingles. He had talked to Frankie who told him of her house as well as Tony's house. Tony of course would not ask for help. She was on twelve hour shifts with the hospital, and could not take off. Tony had repaired her roof, but did not have shingles. The windows were replaced, her house was in good shape. His was a disaster.

"You should text Frankie, and tell her we should be there in two days."

"Already done."

Frank, and Jackie arrived at Frankie's house late in the afternoon. They dropped the trailer, and headed for Tony's house since Frankie was not home. She was working from six in the morning till six in the evening. Both sat quiet as they drove through Houston. House, after house had carpet, sheetrock, refrigerators, and other items sitting in piles near the road. They had watched the hurricane on television, and had seen the news reporting the devastation, but to see it was beyond belief. Frank turned on the street heading for Tony's house. He stopped in front of the house seeing Tony dragging a large piece of carpet out of the house sitting it on the pile. Jackie stepped out walking up to him hugging him. "You ok Tony?"

"Yes, It's a chore, good to see you." he was surprised to see them.

Frank shook his hand. "Frankie said you needed help. So we're here. We have a load of shingles for Frankies house. We figured the lumber yards would be running short."

"Yes they are."

"We're here to help, let us know what we can do?"

They followed Tony into the small house. It had a living room, a small kitchen, one bedroom, one bathroom with a single garage, and a back porch.

"I've removed most of the carpet. I was glad to see there are hardwood floors underneath. They are still in good shape so they won't have to be replaced. You can start taking off the sheetrock."

Frank found a hammer in the garage, and began knocking holes in the sheetrock as Jackie, and he ripped it off. When he finished taking out all the carpet Tony began taking out the sheetrock. They worked till five thirty then left for Frankies house.

Frankie was at the house when they arrived, she had made a casserole.

Jackie hugged her "You look tired honey."

"Twelve hour shifts are hard. I work, come home, eat, talk to Tony and go to sleep. The hospital is filled to capacity"

They talked until the evening Frankie went to bed. Frank, and Jackie slept in the second bedroom, and Tony slept on the couch. At five thirty Frankie kissed Tony as he slept. He woke up talking for a short time then Frankie left for the hospital.

Jackie cooked breakfast, then they headed back to Tony's house. John, and April arrived at noon. They ate, and talked of the devastation. John walked through the house inspecting it. He sat with the group eating. When they finished eating he said "I think Frank, Tony, and I should go to Frankie's house, and knock out the shingling. He handed Jackie a small crow bar. "All the nails sticking out of the studs including the ceiling need to be pulled out so we can put the sheetrock up."

Jackie took the crow bar, and began pulling nails. April had set up two sawhorses, and had Frank, and Tony take off the front door placing it on the sawhorses.

"I'll sand it down, and we'll go with a different color." She handed Tony a block of wood with sandpaper, and a stapler. He stapled the sandpaper to the wood for her.

"What's wrong with the color it is."

April smiled, "I'll sand the door since it was damaged by the water, and well the color you had was ugly."

Frank, John, and Tony arrived at Frankie's house at two o'clock. John handed Tony a flat nosed shovel pointing to the roof. "Need to take the rest of the shingles off."

Tony set the ladder against the roof, and grumbled as he went up. Starting at the top of the roof he began to remove the shingles. John handed a hammer to Frank. "Tearing off is the worst part of roofing. You can drive the nails down sticking up."

Frank smiled "I can do that."

John checked out the shingles seeing all the nails, and paper with the shingles was there. He went to the roof checking it out. He found one piece of decking needing replaced. Tony had bought extra decking prior to the storm. He handed the piece of plywood to Frank, and together they removed the rotten decking replacing it.

With the shingles removed Tony carried up the black paper as John, and Frank tacked it down. He began carrying up the shingles which was hard work carrying the heavy bundle up the ladder. John looked at Frank "That's a young man's job."

They had half of the house shingled when Frankie pulled up. She smiled "I like the color of the shingles.

"Your Mother picked out the shingles."

Jackie, and April arrived so the men quit work, and went inside. They talked of the storm, and the work needing done. Frankie said "I need to take a shower. Tony you don't have to wash my back since you're so tired."

They all looked at Tony.

"She's making that up. I have never washed her back while she showered."

Frank was staring at Tony.

"I mean it, I have not seen her shower."

Frankie giggled looking at her Mother, "Isn't he cute when he's embarrassed."

"You need to stop telling stories Frankie tell them I have not, you know." Tony's face was red as Frank stared at him.

"We may have to have a talk Tony." Frank said leaning forward.

Jackie laughed "Ok Frank, and Frankie that's enough. They all laughed as Tony's face was red.

"Well it is good to have someone wash your back." April said looking at John.

"After we were married."

April winked at John. his face was red as he looked at April. She began to giggle as did Frankie, and Jackie.

Frankie went to bed early. April, and John slept on an air mattress in the living room. That morning as she was going to work Frankie kissed Tony.

"You know you're not very funny telling stories."

Frankie giggled Ok I'll behave.

Jackie, and April went to Tony's house as Frank, John, and Tony put the shingles on. They finished the shingles by three. John, and Frank went to Tony's house to begin wiring it, while Tony stayed, and put on the cap. Cutting the shingles, and laying them across the peak, and seams was tedious work. He finished as the others came home. John looked at Tony as he was cleaning up the job. "I'm glad you're not a fireman."

Chapter IX

John looked at the old breaker box in the garage. He shook his head saying

"I haven't seen a box like this for years."

"My Dad had one close to this, he kept boxes of these old glass screw in fuses."

John looked at Frank "I don't doubt it since they would blow constantly. I'm going to keep it, and take it home. My son Ricky sometimes teaches at the VoTech, he can use this as an example of ancient electricity.

John removed the fuse box and put in a new one. He finished wiring the small house, then he, and Frank began putting on the sheetrock. Tony on the steep roof carefully removed the shingles which was hard work since it had three layers. The roof was so steep he had to nail two by fours on the roof to stand on while he worked. When he finished he removed the rotting plywood. John, and Frank helped him put on the decking.

Tony sat outside leaning against the house, he was exhausted. Frank came outside, taking a bottle of water from the cooler sitting beside him.

"I remember now why I'm a mechanic, and not a carpenter. That taping, and bedding is a pain."

Tony laughed, "that's why I decided to go to college in California."

They sat for a while when Tony sat up. He took a deep breath "Frank I think Frankie is the greatest thing that has ever happened to me. I love her, and I swear I will always take care of her. I would like your permission to marry her. Your approval, and blessing is important to me."

Tony felt like he was about to pass out. He looked at the big man with the full beard he respected. John had stopped at the door when he heard Tony speaking. He bowed his head, and prayed.

"Two things, first Frankie is special, she is my only daughter who I love more than my life. I want your promise that you will always take care of her."

"I promise."

"She can be difficult, she has a temper, strong willed to the point of stubborness. You are going to have to be firm. I want her to marry a christian man, and you are him. I give you my permission, and my blessing."

Tony let out a deep breath.

"Second," Frank sat up staring at Tony. "What took you so long to ask?

"I was scared."

John let his breath out. He walked out of the house going to the cooler for a bottle of water. He smiled "The bedding is actually not bad. I can go over it, and feather it so it looks good."

Frank smiled "you don't lie well. I know the mudding is pretty bad"

'It's not that bad. I figure the gals will be back soon. I'm glad April could find a lumber yard with the materials we need to finish up."

"It's good for Jackie, and April to go seventy five miles. Give them some woman time together." Frank said as he drank the bottled water.

"And out of my hair." John laughed while drinking his water.

Frank looked at John "Tony finally asked for Frankies hand. I gave him my blessing."

John grinned "Good" he shook Frank, and Tony's hand. "I was hoping he would ask, I was afraid she would be asking me for my blessing."

The men laughed.

"I haven't asked her yet, I will soon."

"Don't wait too long" Frank said, "She does not have a lot of patience. She may ask you."

Jackie, and April pulled up with the trailer.

"I told you they would be sitting here goofing off." Jackie said as she walked to the cooler getting two bottles of water.

"Hey now this is my first break." Frank said, frowning.

April drank the water Jackie handed her. "We were able to get everything. The cabinets may be a little long, but you can cut them to fit. Jackie picked out a pretty color for the house, and matched the shingles."

"I was going to paint the house white."

"I know" Jackie said "But it will be grey with white trim. I'll talk to Frankie, She's a good painter. Oh by the way the inside will not be white. I bought some nice colors for inside."

Tony did not argue.

John stood up "Ok Frank, and I will hang the cabinets while Tony is putting on the shingles."

"Sounds good to me," Frank said standing up.

The following evening the roof was shingled, the cabinets hung, Jackie, and April sanded the floors with a rented sander, and the walls were painted. It was late when they finished heading for Frankies house. John explained the only thing left was to paint the outside. Frankie said she was off the next three days, and she would be glad to help Tony finish up. The family spent the evening sitting outside talking.

Tony holding Frankie's hand said "I called NASA telling them I was ready to come back to work. They told me to stay home since they are dealing with their own issues due to the storm. I volunteered to come in, they said no."

Frankie giggled "Are you having a rough time honey?"

"I almost forgot how much fun it was to work with Dad."

The following morning as Frank maneuvered out of the Houston traffic, and into the open country, he relaxed. He smiled looking at Jackie.

"Tony ask for Frankie's hand.

Jackie smiled "was he nervous?"

"I thought he was going to pass out."

Jackie laughed "the poor guy, I feel sorry for him having to face you."

Frank laughed "Now I'm not that bad."

Jackie held his hand "No, honey you really are not. But you sure have your bluff in."

"I gave him my blessing."

John, and April heading north cruised in the light traffic when they left Houston. Looking straight ahead John said "Tony ask Frank for his blessing to marry Frankie,"

April looked anxiously. "Frank gave his blessing."

April smiled as the tears formed in her eyes. "Good I was hoping he would."

"I told him not to wait too long, or she would be asking him.

April giggled.

Frankie, and Tony scraped, and painted the house in three days. Tony was pleased with the grey with white trim. The shingles were a dark grey which made the house look great. Tony holding Frankies hand said "Go home, and clean up I'll take you out on the town."

Tony arrived at seven, Frankie looked great in a nice dress, her hair, and nails done. They went to a nice restaurant in Houston on the waterfront. When they finished eating they walked holding hands on the wharf. At the end of the wharf as they looked at the full moon. Tony on one knee proposed. Frankie smiling said yes.

Chapter X

Jackie picked up the cell phone, her smile grew broader as she looked at the text from Frankie. "Tony proposed, and Frankie said yes."

Frank grinned "Good."

April was not sure who the text was from not recognizing the number. She put her hand to mouth as she read Tony had asked her to marry, and she said yes. She left the greenhouse immediately going into where John was watching the game. She sat on his lap. "Tony proposed, and Frankie said yes."

John hugged April.

After church Frankie followed Tony home. She always drove herself to church. Sitting at the table eating Tony said "I have an idea. Your parents have invited me to come over for Thanksgiving. Why don't we go? On Christmas if you're parents don't have plans they could fly with us to Salem for Christmas with my family."

Frankie smiled "I love it. Dad, and Mom don't make big plans since I've been away, and Roger, and Jody go to her family's house for Christmas. They are wealthy, and usually travel somewhere for Christmas."

When the dishes were finished Tony holding Frankies hand walked into the living room sitting on the small couch.

"I need to talk to you about something." He sat quietly for a while. "The shuttle is almost complete. We have been working hard on getting it ready for its flight to the Space Station. The new Director has been pushing hard for us to take our own ship rather than rely on the

Russians. He wants the shuttle program to be a success. January third is the date of lift off. I have been chosen to be on the mission."

Frankie sat quiet looking at Tony. Her voice just above a whisper asked, "how long will you be gone?"

"Six months."

She stood up walking to the center of the room. Her head was spinning. She turned facing Tony. "I was wanting to get married in May. Now you will be gone six months!"

She turned walking through the kitchen out the backdoor. She stood on the small deck Tony had built. She stayed outside by herself for a while, as Tony sat inside the house. She walked in taking Tony's hand. He stood up as she hugged him.

"I'm sorry for being selfish. I don't want you gone for six months. I like having you close." she stepped back looking at him. "I will wait for you. September is not too bad in Tucson. It would be a good time to marry."

Tony smiled "Ok, I'll miss you, but we can skype.

They sat on the couch together. "Have you told your Mother?"

"No, I wanted to talk with you. I'll call tonight."

Frankie drove home her emotions in a turmoil. She talked to Jackie who said she would like to go to Salem for Christmas, and looked forward to seeing her, and Tony for Thanksgiving. Jackie reassured Frankie as she cried on the phone telling about Tony going to the Space Station.

April answered the phone.

"Mom, is Dad there I need to talk to both of you so can you put the phone on speaker."

"Is everything ok Tony" What's wrong?"

Nothings wrong Mom I have some news I want to tell you both."

"It's not Frankie is it? Oh honey is it the wedding?"

"Mom please, Frankie is great, no problems. Please put Dad on the phone.

"Ok honey." She walked quickly into the room where John was watching television. "Tony is on the phone, he wants to speak to both of us."

John turned off the television. April looking at the cell phone. "I think this is the speaker button. Hello, Tony can you hear me?"

"Yes Mom am I on speaker?"

"Yes I can hear you son." John answered.

Tony took a deep breath. "Couple of things. Frank, and Jackie have invited Frankie, and I to Thanksgiving. I'm going to Tucson with Frankie. I was thinking since my Cessna has four seats. I thought it would be nice to have Frank, and Jackie come with me, and Frankie home for Christmas."

"That's a wonderful idea Tony. We expected you might be with Frankie at her parents house for Thanksgiving. That's part of being together. Deciding on the holidays."

"Your Mother is right" Frank said leaning toward the phone sitting on the automon. "We will miss seeing you for Thanksgiving. Christmas with you, and Frankie with Frank, and Jackie will be great."

"I thought you would be ok with the plan. Also the shuttle is almost finished. The lift off date is January third. I have been selected to be on the mission to the Space Station."

There was a silence on the phone. April put her hand to her mouth as she stood up walking off. Tears began to come to her eyes.

"Is that something you want to do son?" John asked, "have you spoken to Frankie?"

"Yes, I talked with her this afternoon, she was not happy. She was wanting to get married in May. She said we can look at September for the wedding. She supports me, but I don't think she likes the idea of me being gone six months."

April walked back to the phone. "Tony are you sure this is a good idea, I mean you have a fiance, and, and a good life."

Tony could hear the emotion in her voice. "Mom I helped build the shuttle, I can work on the space station, and I want to go."

"Ok honey." April whispered.

"It's good to hear from you son. Tell Frank, and Jackie we look forward to seeing them on Christmas. You know how much your Mother loves Christmas."

"Ok Dad I will, and Mom please don't worry. I'll talk to you later."

John hung up the phone. He walked to April hugging her.

"Your son is an engineer, and an astronaut, and astronaut's go to space."

Chapter XI

Tony spent long hours at NASA working on the shuttle. All of NASA concentrated their efforts on finishing the Shuttle for the January third lift off. Tours of dignitaries were held including the Governor of Texas, with state Representatives, and Senators. Congressmen from the Federal Government toured NASA. The President called wanting updates on the mission.

Janet Grace was selected as Commander for the mission. She was an experienced astronaut who had been to the Space Station twice. She insisted Jordan Markly, to be assigned as the pilot, Linda Kim, and Tony were both engineers who were experienced, and capable. She sat in the conference room knowing the federal Senators were not in favor of using the outdated Space Shuttle. They made it clear it was more economical to use the Russian rockets. She patiently answered their questions, watched as the director as well as the delegation from Texas made their case for the U.S. to stop relying on the Russians. The Russians were difficult to get along with, and often did not listen to NASA, and would limit the number of astronauts who could fly. The U.S. was sending money to Russia supporting their space program, in addition to engineers, and other men and women to help.

Senator Howlk who was chairman of the powerful finance budget committee listened to the presentation. Speaking to the Director said "I have to look at the cost of how much this country will spend on refitting an older shuttle. It's more economical to continue with the Russians." He looked at Janet, "I see you are politically correct with a white woman, a Black man, an Asian woman, and a white boy."

"I find that offensive, if you are making a joke it's in poor taste Senator. This crew was chosen for ability, and experience, race had nothing to do with it sir!"

Senator Howlk was obviously upset. He was a man who was powerful, and knew it. He was not used to being challenged. His eyes quickly darted to the journalist in the room.

"Now commander, don't be so touchy, I was only joking."

Janet stared back at the Senator. She knew he was being demeaning. She sat quietly as the Director quickly changed the subject speaking of the qualifications of the crew.

When the tour was concluded the Director called his top team to his office. He was upset with Janet for challenging Senator Howlk. She sat quietly as he let her know she could jeopardize the mission by showing disrespect to the Senator.

Janet stood up, anger apparent on her face.

"Replace me, I won't step down, and if you want to fire me you go ahead, Director. The man is a racist!" She immediately walked out of the room.

The following day journalist reported the comment by Senator Howlk. He was blasted in the media. The Director of NASA nor the Governor would comment on the statement. Senator Howlk's office released a statement apologizing for the comment stating the joke was in poor taste. He was not happy.

The Director sat with Janet talking, explaining he had to balance the needs of NASA, and his personal opinion. He did not like the comment, and also did not like the idea of having to please the arrogant Senator who did control their future. Janet acknowledged his position was tough. She did not apologize. She would remain as Commander.

Tony was glad for the Thanksgiving break. He, and Frankie flew to Tucson for Thanksgiving with Frank, and Jackie. The house was crowded with the large family. Roger, and Jody with their son. Frank's mother, along with Jackie's parents. Brothers, and sisters attending with their children, it was a full house. All of them wanted to meet Tony who was engaged to Frankie. He explained his job, and the family was excited about him going into space. It was a good break as Tony met Frankie's family. They were loud, and fun to be around.

The Shuttle was completed in mid December all was ready for lift off. Everything would be checked, and rechecked. Tony, and the other engineers were concerned, and suggested the lift off be postponed since everything had been rushed. The mission would not be rescheduled.

Tony checked the long range forecast before leaving. The weather would be perfect for flying. The Christmas gifts were mailed to Salem so they would not have to be taken on the small plane. It was a pleasant flight. With Frank, and Jackie sitting behind Tony, and Frankie. When they touched down Tony taxied off the main runway heading for the hangers. When he turned off the plane he looked back saying "Mom is really big into Christmas. It's her favorite time of the year."

Frank, and Jackie nodded without speaking. The luggage was unloaded, and they soon saw John walking towards them. He hugged Frankie "how was the flight?"

"Great."

John shook hands with Frank, and Jackie. They walked toward the main building where Tony made arrangements for the plane.

Placing the luggage in the back seat of the SUV. Frank said he had borrowed Sissy's vehicle to accommodate everyone. Frank sat in the front seat, as Jackie, and Frankie sat in the second seat. Tony sat in the back with the luggage.

"I'm used to sitting in the back." Tony said sitting back. They others smiled.

Frank gave them a tour of the city explaining April would want to take them, and the grandchildren on a tour in the evening showing them the Christmas Lights. When they arrived Frank, and Jackie were impressed with the cabin. There were lights on the outside of the house, and a strand of lights followed the curve of the circle drive. It was not much. April came out of the house as the luggage was unloaded. She hugged Frankie, Tony, Jackie, and Frank. Walking up the steps April said "hold on to the rail. I have some apple cider inside."

"Also coffee." Frank said as he followed the group.

April looked back at him frowning.

They each complied. John held the door open as the others walked inside. They were stunned as the house looked like a picture of a christmas village. A huge tree with presents stacked under it. A train with cars attached was circling the tree. Angels, bears with christmas hats, elves, Santa, and Mrs Claus sitting in rocking chairs near the window. A large beautiful nativity scene on the fireplace mantel. It was a winter wonderland, and it was more than any had expected. Frank followed John up the stairs where he went into a room which was also decorated. He sat the luggage down "Nice." he said looking at the christmas scene in the bedroom.

"Yes," John said "the whole house. To answer the question you are thinking." We will be giving tours in the evening as people love coming here seeing April's decoration."

The kitchen, and living room were decorated with nutcracker's of all sizes, Christmas villages, and lights hanging throughout the house. April served them apple cider in decorative cups with a stick of cinnamon in the cider. Everyone was in awe not sure what to say.

April was excited telling them they would go to a community choir this evening. And they could see the christmas lights. Her eyes glistened in excitement as she talked.

They talked of their families, and the wedding. April asked if she could help since she had three weddings she had worked on.

Jackie said "I would love to have your help."

When the talk turned to Tony going in space April left, going into the kitchen. She brought out more apple cider, then walked back into the kitchen. She was upset.

Frankie came into the kitchen "would it be ok if Mom sees your amazing Greenhouse's?"

"Yes of course."

Jackie was impressed with the greenhouse. She, and April talked of the oils, and the beneficial uses for each one. Jackie was impressed with the extent of April's knowledge of herbs, and their uses.

The family gathered at a large park where lights with christmas scenes were sat up. They laughed as the children looked in awe of all the lights, and the different scenes. Different groups performed for the large crowd singing traditional Christmas Carols as well as more modern songs. April frowned when Sissy gave her daughters hot cocoa with marshmallows floating on top.

"Be careful there's a lot of sugar in cocoa."

"I know mom, but the girls don't like coffee"

"Don't get smart." Sissy giggled.

They drove through the city looking at the Christmas light arriving late in the evening. They sat eating peanut butter cookies with no extra sugar added. As it grew late they went to their rooms. Tony laying in bed heard the door open. Frankie came in on her tiptoes. She sat on his bed wearing a christmas tee shirt. She put her hand on his face kissing him. He put his arms around her whispering "are you my gift I can unwrap."

She giggled as he nibbled her ear. "Oh, be careful you will be on Santa's naughty list." She kissed him then tiptoed out of his room.

John with his sons, and grandsons along with Frank went fishing. It was a cool day, the river had Ice but had not frozen over. The women went shopping. They had a great time fishing. They were able to bring in salmon, chinook, and steelhead. Frank had never fished for salmon, and had a great time. When they returned the fish were cleaned. John put the remains of the fish in a pile near the green house for it to be used as organic fertilizer. April baked the fish adding herbal seasoning. It was good, Frank, and Jackie was surprised how good it was. In the evening groups of children with parents showed up at the house. The children looked in wonder at the house.

On Sunday which was Christmas Eve. April wore a red dress trimmed in white fur she had a small red Beret on her head.

Frankie giggled "You look like Mrs. Claus."

"No, I look better."

The service was festive with Christmas Carols being sung. Frank with his deep baritone voice, and Jackie's alto voice sang out. Frankie also sang loud. April smiled as she listened to the beautiful voices. When the preacher spoke Jackie would say "Amen, Praise God!"

Others in the congregation would look at her, and some smiled. When it was over the men, and women congratulated Tony, and Frankie. Many of them excited Tony was going on the shuttle into space.

When dinner was completed Jackie, Frankie and April sat talking about the wedding. Jackie reached over holding April's small hand, she looked directly at her saying "April you need to face the fact Tony is going into space."

April sat quietly then said, speaking just above a whisper "I'm so scared, so many things could go wrong."

"That's why God has given each person a measure of Faith. The Lord said, "What good does it do to worry."

April closed her eyes "I try, I do pray, but I feel so overwhelmed with fear."

"I do too," Frankie said, "so does Mom, and Dad, I would guess John, but you have to put your faith in Jesus."

April wiped her eyes "I'm trying." She stood up "we should join the men So close to Christmas I would hate for them to get put on the naughty list."

The following morning after breakfast all the family gathered in the living room. John with a Santa Hat, and April wearing her beret handed out christmas presents. It was a fun time as Jackie called Roger, and Jody on skype. She introduced the family to them as they all greeted them saying "Merry Christmas!"

April played the piano as the family sang. They had all natural snacks, and apple cider, coffee, and tea was also available.

Tony, and Frankie would leave late in the morning with Frank, and Jackie. John, and April drove them to the airport. They walked to the plane, and as Tony went through his pre flight preparations, April hugged them telling them to write. She hugged Tony, and walked quickly to the main building. John watched as the plane took off flying southeast. He walked into the airport. Holding April's hand walking out to the building saying "Tony's a good pilot."

Chapter XII

The shuttle shook violently as it lifted off shrugging off the bounds of Earth. Fire, and smoke poured from the bottom of the rocket as it moved quickly through the air. April closed her eyes covering her face as she saw the rocket lift off. No one teased her as the family sat watching the lift off. Frankie at the hospital stopped in the lounge watching anxiously.

The shaking stopped as the shuttle left the atmosphere. Jordan steared it towards the space station after it had orbited the Earth. The shuttle docked, the door opened, and the crew walked onto the International Space Station. They each had assignments, and with six months of the mission ahead of them there was plenty of work.

John, and April watched the NASA channel as Tony, and Linda in space suits moved around the outside of the space station. What the two were doing they did not know. Their son was in space hooked on to a line, and was moving around in outer space. It was hard for April with her fear, but she did watch.

Frankie sitting in her house alone would watch the NASA channel seeing Tony, and the other members of the crew. He had a designated time he could call. So they were able to talk of what was happening. Frankie kept him up on the wedding plans. She had gone home, and her and Jackie had gotten into a fight over the wedding dress. They had narrowed the numerous dresses to two. Frank stepped in telling them both to settle down, and try to enjoy the time together. Jackie said both dresses were nice, and she could pick out her dress. She would agree with her decision. Jackie was a detail person, and she was pretty well driving everyone crazy with the smallest detail. Tony felt relieved that he was not there. He spoke with his parents, and family when he could. He, and the crew stayed busy on the space station, and soon it was time to prepare for the trip home.

It was mid August on a Saturday morning John drinking coffee as April sat quiet drinking her tea. "I'm going to Tucson."

John's eyebrows went up "when?"

"Sunday, I want to help with the wedding. Jackie is getting overwhelmed with planning, and I want to help her. I do have experience you know."

John sat quiet looking at April. He chose his words carefully.

"Are you planning on driving to Tucson?"

"NO, I'M GOING TO FLY. Tony should be home in a couple weeks, and the wedding is September tenth. I know the last few weeks are the most difficult. You will be fine without me. So will you make the arrangements for me. I'm going to pack."

John picked up his cell phone calling the Salem airport.

John explained to April as they sat on the seat outside the gate.

"You will fly into Los Angeles airport, have a thirty minute lay over, and arrive at Tucson somewhere around six in the evening. Jackie will pick you up."

April nodded her head as she took a bite of the brownie in her hand.

"Be careful with those." John warned. He knew the brownies were laced with marijuana oil.

April nodded as she fought the fear that was raging inside her.

She stood up as the boarding began. She hugged John, and walked with determination toward the gate. A flight attendant showed her to her seat. She saw a pretty asian woman sitting by the window. A nice looking soldier stood up from his aisle seat allowing her to sit down in the middle seat. He placed her small bag in the overhead compartment. April put her seat belt on, and closed her eyes praying.

The airplane moved slowly. April gasped, and dug her fingers into the armrest.

The young woman asked "are you ok Mam?"

"Okay! I'm strapped inside a tube of thin metal that will be at forty thousand feet traveling at five hundred miles an hour! What could possibly go wrong!"

The woman patted her hand, "we will be fine, I fly all the time, and I promise you we are safe."

April took a deep breath as the airplane began to pick up speed then felt it left off the ground, and yelled "Oh sweet Jesus!"

The soldier put his hand over hers saying "stay calm Mam; we're going to be alright."

"We're off the ground, and flying in the air! We are defying the law of gravity, and tempting the Lord himself!"

The young woman put her hand on April's shoulder "What's your name?"

"April"

"Were you born in April?

April nodded. The young woman said her name was Angela, and talked to her throughout the flight. The soldier told her silly jokes, and talked of his family. April settled down, and ate the rest of her brownie.

The soldier who said his name was Trevor held her hand saying "the plane is about to descend, we will be fine April I promise you."

"My God in heaven we're falling!" April screamed as the plane started down.

Trevor tried to comfort her as she felt a rumbling under her feet. April started crying. Angela told her it was the wheels coming down.

When the wheels touched down April said "Thank You Jesus!"

The plane taxied to the gate. April stood up on shaking legs as Trevor helped her stand. She walked off the plane in a daze. Angela told her how to get to the other side of the airport where her gate was. She held her hand pointing to the stairs going down. Saying "all you have to do is step onto the tram, and listen as the woman tells of each gate. Yours is seventy-one, so get off on seventy-one. Now if you miss it, just stay on, and it will come back around."

April hugged Angela then walked down the steps holding on to the rail, and her small carry on bag.

When the tram stopped she stepped on as the door opened. She sat down, and as it moved quickly she heard a woman's voice over the speaker. "Gates fifteen through Twenty-five. She concentrated as the tram would slow the woman's voice would call out the gate numbers. As the train slowed she heard "gates sixty-five through seventy-five."

Two women who were talking, April looked at them asking "is this gate seventy-one?"

One woman looked at her with a disgusted look "yes it is" she said sarcastically.

April stood up as the tram slowed.

"You should use a natural moisturizer honey. The one you are using isn't working for you."

She stepped off the tram when the doors opened. She turned looking at the woman who looked at her with a hateful, disgusted look. April gave her the finger. Turning around saying to herself out loud "Be sure to scrub real hard with a cactus."

April found the gate, reading the board saying Tucson. She walked to the desk as a woman helped a man in front of her. When he walked off April laid the ticket down on the counter. "This is the gate for Tucson?"

The woman smiled "yes it is."

"Do I need to check in, or do anything?"

"No." The woman said looking at the ticket "you are good to go. We will be boarding in twenty minutes."

"Thank you, and can you tell me where the bathroom is?'

"Down the hall on your right."

April sat the top lid down on the toilet, and sat on it. She looked through her bag taking out a bottle. She removed a rolled up cigarette, and a book of matches. She smoked half of the marijuana cigarette.

She walked slowly back to the gate. Sitting quietly April prayed trying to get a control of the fear that swept over her. She was distracted by a noise. She saw a very large woman sitting in a chair with a small dog. It looked to her like a Chihuahua. April stared at the woman who held the small dog close to her face. The small dog was barking, and yelping excitedly. The large woman was saying "who's a good dog. Who's the best dog ever? You're so pretty, yes you are!"

April felt sick to her stomach watching the scene of the large woman talking silly to the dog who was licking her face, and barking excitedly. She said after a short while.

"Mam that's not sanitary."

The woman sat the dog down looked angrily at April, Screaming at her "you don't tell me what is sanitary my Pookie is clean, no doubt cleaner then you!"

The man sitting next to the large woman who was much bigger, and wedged into the chair began yelling. "You mind your own business Lady. Pookie is my wife's emotional support dog. No one cares what you think!

April raised her voice "Your Pookie was liking its butt earlier."

The large woman became hysterical. Screaming, and crying, as she sat the small dog on her lap. The large man was yelling, and trying to get out of the chair he was wedged into. April looked at the two not sure if she should laugh, or run. So she said

"That dog was liking its butt, and you let it lick your face. That is not sanitary!"

The woman became more hysterical crying, and yelling. The large man was able to get out of his chair, pointing at April, and screaming at her to shut up, and mind her own business. The people in the area were snickering, and some stared at the two large people screaming. Security officers soon showed up, two of them talked to the large man, and woman who was wailing, and crying loudly. A security officer walked up to April asking "what's going on here?"

April stood up as did a woman, and man next to her. April explained "the woman was allowing the small dog to lick her face which is disgusting. And the dog had been licking its butt. The lady freaked out, and became hysterical."

The woman, and man verified her story saying the large woman was loud, and disgusting.

The officer stepped back trying not to laugh. He walked to the other two men who said the small dog was an emotional support dog. And the woman was upset about being insulted. The security officers talked to the man, and woman telling them they would have to settle down, or be escorted out. The large man started to argue. The officer held up his hand saying "Any more outburst, and both of you will be escorted out."

The man's face was beat red as the woman continued to cry. He walked to April "I would appreciate it if you did not speak to the couple who are upset."

April nodded her head sitting back.

The Officer told all of the people in the area to please not upset the woman with the emotional support animal.

When it was time to board April walked to the gate, and boarded the plane. A flight attendant helped her find her seat. As it taxied away from the gate she was subdued, but said loudly as it lifted off "Oh sweet Jesus!"

The plane landed as April was praying. The captain announced "We have landed in Tucson, and those who are departing I hope you had a pleasant flight. For those traveling to Dallas please remain seated, and we will leave shortly."

April stood up taking a deep breath. She saw a young man in a Dallas Cowboy Hat sitting in the aisle seat across from her.

She asked "would you help me get my bag?"

He smiled standing up opening the overhead compartment. He handed April her bag saying, "I hope we can make it to Dallas without you, and your prayers Mam."

April patted his face "don't be smart. Thank you."

Walking through the rows of seats she entered first class. She stopped seeing the large man, and woman sitting, both glaring at her. She pointed to the woman's lap. They looked at the small Chihuahua sitting on the woman's lap liking its butt. The woman immediately became hysterical crying loudly. April continued to walk leaving the plane hearing the hysterical woman.

April hugged Jackie tightly. They picked up her luggage then left the airport. "Could we get something to drink. I would like some ice tea."

Jackie stopped at a sonic ordering two unsweet iced teas. When it arrived April took the tea taking a drink, she sat it down, reached in her pocket taking out the half smoked cigarette, lit it. Jackie was surprised watching April.

"Medicinal only honey, I just defied the laws of gravity, and survived the most harrowing experience of my life, exception being childbirth.Want a hit?"

Jackie took the cigarette, inhaled, handing it back. It was strong. April inhaled on the cigarette that was now almost gone. She threw it out the window as a police car pulled in next to them.

"We should probably go now." April said rolling up the window.

The following week April helped Jackie with the wedding. She organized the flowers. She bought several fake flowers from WalMart, and the dollar store to supplement the flowers from the florist. Jackie was surprised how beautiful the fake flower bouquets were. They arranged the real flowers, and fake flowers at the church as they decorated it for the wedding. Frankie came for the weekend, and was amazed how calm her mother was with April there. She had helped not only with the wedding, but helped Jackie to settle down. Frankie left on Sunday afternoon knowing Tony was scheduled to arrive home in two days They would be married in a week.

Chapter XIII

"Houston we have a problem!" Commander Grace's voice was controlled

"we've lost power" the transmission stopped. Ground control watched in horror, without power the shuttle fell from the sky like a brick. There was nothing they could do. Many began to pray, these who believed as well as those who didn't. All they could do was watch helplessly.

Tony unbuckled his seat belt, and ran for the side of the shuttle. He removed the panels as the ship filled with smoke. He grabbed the lever, and pulled opening the vents manually. Smoke began to clear out. He looked at the burnt wires, and began to pull them out. Using his multi tool he started stripping the wires of its coating. Linda removed panels as Tony yelled "the black, and green!"

She immediately began searching "we're ok.

Tony began rewiring the burnt wires. He ran for the back of the shuttle removing panels, began to work on the wires, and moving pipes. The back of the ship was filled with smoke. He choked, and coughed, his eyes burned. A fire flamed up as Tony was screwing in a pipe. It burned, but he could not stop until he finished. As he started back he felt the ship was pointing down. He made it back to the panel, and began to quickly wire the loose burnt wire. He looked at Linda nodding unable to speak as he coughed. Linda turned toward the front yelling "Now! Hit it now!"

Commander Grace hit the button as the engine whined then roared to life. Linda heard a loud noise seeing sparks fly out hitting

Tony knocking him back. Jordan slowly pulled the nose up as the ship was sluggish.

"Houston power partially restored! Wheels are locked, they won't deploy. We're bringing the ship down on its belly!"

Fire Trucks on the runway immediately began to spray foam on the runway.

As they approached the ground Jordan tried to slow the ship.

"Parachutes now!"

Commander Grace tried, but the parachutes wouldn't open. She turned looking at Linda who was checking on Tony.

"The chutes won't deploy!"

Linda ran for the back of the shuttle through the smoke she found the panel. She opened it, grabbed the leaver, and pulled down. The parachutes flew out, and when they caught wind the shuttle slowed immediately. The force of the slowing shuttle threw Linda backwards. She hit hard on the door jamb, and bounced off. The nose of the shuttle went down as the parachutes opened. Jordan fought the temptation to jerk the stick back. He slowly brought the nose up as it approached the ground.

Frankie in the hospital lounge stood shocked as she saw the shuttle falling. The reporter was scared, and excited saying something was wrong as it fell. Her hand on her mouth she stared in disbelief. Tammy Shaw, a twenty five year veteran of the Houston police force who had retired, and worked security for the hospital, put her arm around Frankie.

April was watching with Frank, and Jackie, she stood up staring at the television as she saw the shuttle falling. Frank stood up putting his arm around April. She turned putting her arms around his neck as his arms were around her, and Jackie. April buried her head in Frank's chest crying. Jackie held onto Frank with her hand on April's shoulder.

John sat forward in his chair. Ricky, Bobby, Sissy with their families had come to the log cabin to watch the shuttle land. They sat in shock watching the shuttle fall. John stood up, his fist clenched.

"Fix it Tony, I know you can."

The world had seemed to stop as the shuttle fell from the sky. All prayed as the horror unfolded before them. When the parachutes deployed, and the nose of the plane came up slowly it hit hard on the pavement throwing sparks as it slid on the underside with no wheels. It stopped as the firetrucks raced for the shuttle.

Commander Grace ran for the door opening it. She turned running for Linda who lay face down. Jordan stumbled over debris as smoke began to fill the ship. The adrenaline, shock, and excitement raced through him. He pulled the fallen panels off Tony, dragging him to the door. He turned as he bumped into someone. A fireman grabbed Tony's arm as another one grabbed his other arm. They dragged him to the door as a fireman taking Jordan to the door. Others were putting out the fire. Tony, and the rest of the crew was loaded onto a helicopter which lifted off heading for the hospital.

April's phone rang. Frank sat her on the couch as she answered.

"The shuttle is down, and Tony is going to be alright April. You have to believe, and have faith."

"I do John, I do."

Frank took the phone from April. "John we'll meet you in Houston. I will get April there. You be strong, and have faith."

"I will."

John looked at Sissy who was crying. She reached into her pocket taking out her cell phone. John went to his room to pack. When he came down Sissy said "your flight leaves in two hours. You should arrive in Houston about six."

Frankie turned going to the elevators. She stopped on the first floor going to the emergency room. When she walked in Dr. Owens walked up to her putting his hand on her shoulder. "The helicopter should be here soon. When it arrives Sherry, William, and I will take care of Tony. You will not."

Frankie nodded knowing the rules. Family was not to work on family.

The helicopter landed, and the crew was brought in. Frankie felt the emotions raise in her seeing Tony with an oxygen mask on an EMT saying "he's in defib!"

She turned her attention to Linda who was on a gurney. She followed the gurney into a room. She had a cut, and bruised shoulder, with smoke inhalation. She checked out Janet, and Jordan. They both had bruises on their chest where the seatbelt dug into them. When she finished she walked to the room where Tony was. Dr. Owens walked out putting his hands on her shoulders.

"He's alive, a severe burn on his hand, smoke inhalation, a slight concussion, and he's been electrocuted. I got this Frankie. We're taking him to ICU."

She only nodded as she watched Tony wheeled out of the emergency room. Tammy stepped up to her.

"I'll take you to the ICU waiting room."

"We want to go."

Frankie turned to see Janet, Jordan, and Linda standing behind her. She nodded as she walked out.

In the waiting room she called Jackie telling her Tony was alive, and his issues. She called John who was on the way to the Airport. She sat back quietly praying as the family of the crew began to show up.

Chapter XIV

Frankie received a text from Jackie they would arrive at the Houston airport at two-forty-five. Frank would land at six-ten. She sat back, her head spinning. She watched as a young man walked in. He talked to the crew asking if they were ok, or if they needed anything. He sat down next to Frankie "I'm Brent from NASA if there is anything you need please ask."

"My parents, and Tony's mom will be at the airport at two-forty-five."

"I'll pick them up." He stood up walking out.

Frankie stood up walking out of the waiting room heading for the double doors of ICU. When she walked in she saw Helen, a nurse who had been at the hospital twenty years.

She looked at Frankie "no, you know the rules, family only, and I'm sorry fiancee is not family." She picked up some papers. "I have to go to personal, and deliver these time sheets. I will be gone for fifteen minutes." She walked past Frankie going out the double doors saying over her shoulder "room five."

Frankie walked around the corner seeing nurses who looked at her then looked down at their computer screens. She smiled knowing all the time sheets were on the computer. She walked to room five seeing Tony laying in bed with a full oxygen mask on. She checked the monitors seeing his heart rate was normal. Dr. Owens had shocked his heart back to normal rhythm. She saw his hand was wrapped up, and the IV in his arm. She leaned over kissing him on the forehead.

"I like to sneak into your room, and see you Tony."

She talked to him, and watched the monitor when she felt a hand on her shoulder.

"Time to go Frankie."

She looked at Helen. She kissed Tony on the forehead, and followed Helen out. Helen held the door for Frankie as she walked out, and to the waiting room. She sent a text to her parents, and John.

April ran into the waiting room hugging Frankie. She hugged the crew as she was introduced to them. Frank, and Jackie sat down as Frankie told them of Tony's condition. April smiled "prayer was answered."

Brent said he would go back to the airport, and pick up Frank. April asked how the crew were feeling, and how they felt. They had bumps, and bruises. Jordan's wife Candice was six months pregnant, and their four year old son was restless. She looked at the cut on Linda's back, and patted her two year old son on the head. She opened her bag, and digging through it found a small round glass container. She pulled LInda's shirt down in the back, and applied the ointment on her cut.

"This will help much better than what the hospital has given you."

She put the bandage back on Linda. She had Jordan pull up his shirt, and applied the ointment on his bruise She took hold of Janet's hand leading her to the bathroom where she applied the ointment on her. When they returned Dr. Owen came in giving them an update on Tony.

"He is resting now. He has a burn on his hand, some smoke inhalation which I believe is not too serious. There could be some scaring. He has a concussion. So he will be here for at least two days. I expect him to wake up tomorrow."

April handed the glass jar to Dr. Owens "this ointment is aloe, and other natural ingredients. You should apply this to his burn."

He smiled taking the jar. "I'll make sure it is applied."

April walked to the vending machine frowning as she looked at the selection.

"Frank, do you have any cash? I left my wallet in my luggage. Which we left on the van." She pointed saying "buy those oreos."

Frank was surprised, but he put his dollar in buying the cookies. April walked to the sink taking a paper towel then walked back digging into her bag. She removed a small glass bottle, and a small pocket knife. Frank handed her the cookies which had six in the package.

They all watched curiously as she opened the package taking out a cookie. She seperated it, and placed two drops on the cookie.

"This is oil extracted from organically grown marijuana. I realize it's not legal in Texas, guns, and alcohol is. Everyone owns a satellite dish so they can watch things that should not be seen, but don't legalize a natural plant created by the Lord." She handed half of the cookie to Jordan. "This will help with the pain, and settle your nerves. You're still in shock honey."

Tammy turned going out the door laughing.

He looked at the cookie. Frankie smiled "I would go ahead, and take it Jordan."

He took the cookie, and ate it. April picked up the other half, and with her small pocket knife scraped off the white filling.

"This is pure sugar which is not good for you." she said looking at Jordan's son. "I hope you are not allowing him too much sugar." she said looking at Jordan.

She placed two drops on the cookie handing it to Janet. She hesitated then accepted it.

April took another cookie separating it, placing two drops on the cookie handing it to Linda. She scraped off the filling, and placed two drops on it giving it to Frankie.

She also gave cookies to Frank, and Jackie.

April stood up handing a cookie to Jordan's son, and Linda's son "I suppose this one time won't hurt anything." She took Frankies hand saying "I want to see Tony."

They walked into the ICU as Helen looked down. They walked to room five.

Frank arrived at six thirty. He went to see Tony then came back in sitting down. As the group sat quiet Linda said "I'm not sure how he did it. Somehow Tony was able to get the engines going. He somehow bypassed the main controls."

"I'm glad he did." Jordan said, placing his hand on hers. "And you deploying the parachutes."

Janet sat listening, "it was scary for those four minutes. I wasn't sure we would make it."

Frank leaned forward on his arms. "You weren't alone Commander."

She looked at him confused.

"Your crew worked together to bring that shuttle home, but I assure you another crew member was with you. As Tony, and Linda worked to start the engines, Jesus was there. He heard the prayers of all those who watched, in Tucson, Salem, and across the United States, including the world. He heard the prayers, and in those four minutes nothing else mattered, but getting that bird, and your crew home safely. Not the petty arguments of politics, or religion. All that was put aside as God's people prayed."

John stood up going to the window seeing the large group who had gathered in the park next to the hospital. A church youth group had come to pray. When word of the group's prayer vigil had been reported on the news. More people showed up. The Marine reserves standing next to the Texas National Guard, churches from different denominations stood side by side praying.

"I know God gave his only son for the salvation of this world." He sighed leaning on the window. "Who am I to not give my son. If it will bring this world together."

April walked to him standing next to him as Frank, and Jackie, with Frankie looked out the window.

"For four minutes this world stood together; perhaps we can put our petty difference aside for the glory of God." Frank said as he put his hand on John's shoulder as tears silently fell from the big man.

Brent spoke after a while. "NASA has reserved rooms for you at a hotel. It's late I suggest you get some rest."

John turned "I agree."

Frankie said John, and April could stay with her. They politely refuse saying she needed to be with her parents. They told Janet, and her husband, Jordan, and his family, and Linda, and her husband, and son goodbye. April gave Jordan's wife a list of herbs she should take during her pregnancy. They went to the van that was parked by the door.

Brent stopped the van by the door of a hotel, and went in to make sure John, and April were checked in. He left telling them he would pick them up at nine o'clock. He left driving Frankie, and her parents home.

John opened the door to the room, and walked in carrying the luggage. April walked to the bed, pulled the covers back, and as she removed her pony tail holder looked directly at John "I want you to make love to me. I need you to hold me in your strong arms , and tell me you love me."

John walked to her holding her in his arms. "I have always loved you. The first time I saw you holding that Stop The War sign with flowers in your hair, and the thin piece of leather headband. I have always loved you. I still see the young beautiful girl in you." He kissed her as he unzipped her dress.

Chapter XV

The young black woman looked up seeing men with cameras walk into the hotel lobby. She picked up the phone dialing it. When John answered the phone he heard a professional voice "Mr. Pierce this is the front desk. There are members of the media in the lobby. I assume they are here to speak to you, and your wife."

"I would prefer to not speak to the media at this time."

"Okay sir I will take care of it, have a good day.

She phoned security, and when two large men arrived she walked to where the men were sitting up cameras. She smiled "may I help you."

"No, we don't need any help. Thank you."

"May I ask why you are here in the hotel lobby"

No one spoke as they continued to work.

"If you are here to interview Mr., and Mrs Pierce I have spoken to them, and they prefer to not give an interview."

The men continued to work ignoring the woman.

She smiled "This is David, and Brad, they will show you gentlemen out."

"I have a right to be here, and you are aware of freedom of the press."

"You will have to leave, our guests' privacy is this hotel's priority." She turned "David, Brad."

The two men stepped forward. "You'll have to leave, so gentlemen please pick up your equipment, or the police will be called."

Both men moved closer to the men who picked up their equipment, and left. David, and Brad moved them off the property, and stood watching the men as they sat up across the street at McDonalds.

Brent arrived in the van with Frankie, and her parents. He walked inside where the young woman called John telling him his ride was here. She told Brent of the media. John, and April walked directly to the van. Once inside Brent said "you should know the media is prowling around. They no doubt would like an interview. It is up to you, NASA has a public relation department, and they are giving a press conference."

Frankie turned in her seat looking at John, and April.

"The hospital called, Tony has been moved from ICU to the third floor."

April threw up her hands "praise the Lord!" She put her arms around John's broad shoulders. "See honey I told you not to worry."

Everyone in the van laughed.

Brent stopped in front of the hospital directly in front of the front door. Leaving the van several journalists tried to speak to the family. They were blocked by security as the family ignored them walking into the hospital. The elevator stopped at the third floor. The family walked down the wide corridor.

Walking into Tony's room Frankie walked directly to the bed. She leaned over looking into Tony's eyes. He said with a hoarse voice "I told you I would be back"

She kissed him lightly on the lips "on a wing, and a prayer."

April walked to the opposite side of the bed. She took Tony's hand "glad to see you awake. How do you feel?"

"Not too good, my chest hurts, and my hand hurts."

"You don't look too good." John said as he stood beside Frankie.

"He has looked better. I've seen better looking men in a bar fight." Frank said from the end of the bed.

"Don't pay any attention to them Tony. I think you look great." Jackie said, smiling at him.

John said "I suppose in time he will be as pretty as ever." He patted Tony's arm. "Had a rough time for a while did you?"

Tony smiled slightly "I had to hot wire the shuttle, to jump start it."

The family would talk until dinner was served. Tony didn't feel like eating, but with the insistence of the family he did eat some of the bland meal. The shuttle crew arrived, and was glad to see Tony was awake. April sent Sissy, Bobby, and Ricky a text telling them all was good. Jackie texted Jody, and Roger.

Ricky, and Bobby had backed the trailer to the barn next to John's house to unload it. They talked of the next job, and of Tony, and family when Ricky saw a group of vehicles drive into the drive. He walked to the cars followed by Bobby. Several men, and women stepped out of the vehicles. Some of them had cameras on their shoulders. They walked to him all of them speaking at the same time. They asked who they were if they had information on Tony Pierce, what was his condition. The two big men stared at the men when Ricky said "you need to speak to NASA they have people who can answer your questions."

"What about Tony Pierce, how is he doing?"

"You need to leave" Ricky said firmly.

Bobby stepped back calling the sheriff's office.

"Who are you? Why should we leave?" A young man asked sarcastically, shoving a mic in Ricky's face..

Ricky swatted the mic away. He stepped up to the smaller man.

"Are you wearing makeup?" he laughed. The young man's face turned red. "My family is away, and me and my brother are taking care of the place while they are gone. So I will ask you one more time to leave."

The other men with cameras crowded closer. "Can you tell how Tony is doing""

"Leave now!" He said stepping close to the man staring down at him.

Bobby said "the sheriff is on his way so you need to leave."

The young man with a sneer shoved the mic in Ricky's face.

"Has Tony's husband Frankie talked with you?"

Ricky grabbed the man's blazer. "Frankie is a beautiful woman engaged to Tony." He pushed the man hard knocking him to the ground. He stepped closer with Bobby beside him glaring down at the man. Patrol cars pulled into the driveway. A deputy sheriff stepped out quickly walking towards the group.

"Sir, I need you to step away please!:"

The young man jumped up as the camera man continued to film.

Bobby said "these people have been asked to leave."

The Deputy walked up standing in front of Ricky "You will have to leave the premises!"

The camera crews continued to film as some of the journalists walked to their car. The Deputy stepped up to the young man handcuffing him. Another Deputy handcuffed the cameraman Other men continued to film as Highway Patrol handcuffed them. Most of the journalists were now moving toward their vehicles. A young woman was writing on a pad when she was handcuffed, and placed in a Patrol car. They were taken to the Sheriff's office and booked in for Trespassing, and Refusing a direct order of a Law Enforcement Officer. They were all released on a Personal Recognizance Bond. Their hearing would be in three days.

Sissy called to tell John, who called his sons telling them to be calm, and not allow their emotions to dictate their actions.

That evening the news ran the story of the journalist being arrested. There was a protest of violating first amendment rights. A competing network ran the story of how another reporter had insinuated Tony was a homosexual. The reporter was called a homophobe, who was sarcastic, and intentionally trying to provoke Ricky. The reporter apologized saying he thought Frankie was a man's name, and meant no offence to the homosexual community. His apology was not accepted. The network news showed part of the altercation. Some of them said the police were too harsh, and yes the Pierce family had a right to privacy.

Sitting in Tony's room the family watched the morning show. April pointed at John "your sons."

"Our sons"

"They act like you."

Tony laughed "my brothers can give me a hard time, but no one else can. Family."

ON THE MORNING SHOW Senator Howlk said he was concerned with the shuttle program. It was expensive, and with the cost of losing a shuttle he had doubts. Other methods more economical should be explored. He shook his head "my prayers are with the Astronauts, and their families."

April frowned "He's an ass!"

Chapter XVI

Commander Grace sat quietly in the chair of the network studios. NASA had insisted she give an interview. She agreed to talk with a popular morning show. The pretty anchor woman said as she looked into the camera.

"Welcome back we are so pleased to have Commander Janet Grace who was commander of the Shuttle that crash landed recently. Can you tell us what went wrong?" She said turning looking at Janet

"Atlantis was the last shuttle to go to the Space Station. It was retrofitted when the President insisted the United States use our own rockets as opposed to flying on the Russian rockets. You see the Russians are sometimes obstinate, and won't allow Americans to fly when we want. We do go into space on their rockets, but only if they agree. This nation has helped build the Russian space program with millions, and millions of dollars. Our scientists, and engineers are there helping them. The shuttle being retrofitted, which was an older model, was in good shape. The lift off was great. We were able to dock at the space station. On reentry we lost power. Tony Pierce, and Linda Kim were able to jump start the engines. Linda manually pulled the lever releasing the parachutes. Jordan was able to land the shuttle without the wheels down." She leaned forward. "I don't see what went wrong. I see what went right."

"What do you mean what went right? The shuttle crashed!"

"Yes, but Tony, and Linda because of their training, and their education was able to start it. Jordan with nerves of steel was able to land. The firemen, and EMT because of their training, laid down foam, put out the fire on the ship, and helped Tony, and Linda who were hurt. Anytime we go into space we all know the dangers. Congress wanting to save money has decided to use the Russian rockets, building up their space program while the United States lags behind. Now I respect all congressmen, and women. They have tough jobs, and have to make critical decisions every day. The President has been pushing congress to allocate more money for NASA so we are not relying on the Russians. China has a great space program, and they, and Russia will dominate in space. Now I know Congress, and NASA are talking, but you know the American people should also have a voice. They should let congress know their opinion. We can continue to build the Russian program with our expertise of scientists, and engineers, and millions, and millions of tax dollars, or invest in America."

The anchor asked many questions which Janet answered.

Before the interview was over emails were sent to congressmen, and women. A young woman who was a progressive running against Senator Howlk began questioning his integrity. She railed on the good ol boy system, corruption, and asked where the money was really going to the Russians. Was it going to the space program, or into Vladimer Putin's pocket. Journalists called NASA, they were referred to Senator Howlk who was furious. He called the director of NASA screaming at him. The director did not back down. Since it was an election year all the congressmen, and women were bombarded with questions of the space program asking where the money went. When the election ended Senator Howlk won by a narrow margin. He was not happy since he was expected to win by a wide margin. The President also took advantage of the wave of patriotism, and pushed for independence for Americans. His budget was approved with NASA receiving a large budget to immediately begin to build its own rockets. Senator Howlk, had to answer continued questions of the money he approved. The journalist watched his committee closely constantly asking for transparency. The Russians refused to answer questions of the money received from the United States.

Daren Triplett the County District Attorney sent out a press release saying the journalist arrested at the Pierce family home would be charged with Criminal Trespassing a misdemeanor, and Refusing to Obey a Lawful Order from a Law Enforcement officer, also a misdemeanor. The penalty, six months in the county jail, and a five hundred dollar fine on each charge. At the Press Conference held the following day he stood before the group of journalists who had gathered on the courthouse steps.

He said "I would like to make a statement before taking questions. The journalist who invaded the home of the Pierce family were asked to leave the property. Many of the journalists did. Those who refused were ordered by the Sheriff's office to leave, they refused, and were arrested The mistomeners they have been charged with carries a six month in jail, five hundred dollar fine on each count. I plan to ask the judge to enforce the maximum penalty. I respect the first amendment, freedom of speech. However, that does not give the media the right to trample on the rights of the Pierce family, or anyone else. The over zealous media need to learn to respect the rule of law that applies to all our citizens."

He answered the questions from the media who questioned him extensively. He was calm, and confident as he answered their questions. He emphasised he was not seeking retribution for the media not being friendly to his office.

He explained "bad press goes with the job. In his duties he often angers some, while others are pleased." He was in his element as the camera's were on him. He pointed out channel seven news. "A week ago the station manager had a commentary where he complained my office was too eager to make plea deals. He questioned the ability of the fine attorneys who work hard defending this county. However, he is now asking for a plea deal for his journalist, who insulted Tony Pierce, and refused to leave the property when asked. This is a double standard the media preaches against."

Eight lawyers sat in a luxurious conference room of a prominent lawyer. Matt Jackson, an attorney, explained he had spoken with DA Triplett who was cordial, but was planning on pushing the charges, and would seek the maximum for each charge. The lawyers discussed strategy for each of their clients they represented. The first amendment, aggressive law enforcement. The discussion continued as Cheryl Burgraff sat listening. She leaned forward, her hands folded on the table. When the discussion stopped as each lawyer was lost in his thoughts she spoke up.

"Daren Triplett may be an arrogant prick, but he is smart, a good lawyer, and a better politician. Tony Pierce is one of our boys. He was raised here, and is an American Hero. He's a Salem boy. The Pierce family is respected. John Pierce, and his Father, and Grandfather, hell his Great Grandparents crossed the Oregon trail." She stood up pouring herself a glass of water. Sitting down she smiled, "my ex husband was desk Sergeant when big John Pierce walked into the police station. He pushed through the officers, and began beating the DEA, and there were eight of them. He jerked the interrogation room door open, dragged out the two agents, interrogating his wife, and the beatings continued. It took the police force, Sheriff's office, and DEA to wrestle him to the jail cells. He got loose in the bullpen, and he beat those officers until they pushed the big man into a cell. He stood at the bars staring out with his fist clenched. Triplett, and I were young assistant DA "s. He wanted to prosecute John. DA Rushing decided to not charge him although the DEA pushed him. The idea of DEA agents with the Sheriff's office with high powered rifles threatening a young boy in his pajamas. April, and her daughter making cupcakes." She laughed "April asked a Deputy to turn off the oven, and take out her cupcakes!" She giggled. "And he did! Men still talk about that in the coffee shops, and barber shops. Gentlemen Triplett will ride on the reputation of the Pierce family, and on Tony Pierce saving the doomed shuttle." She took a drink sitting the glass down. "Most of your sons were in John's boy scout troop, including mine. I buy supplements from April as do your wifes." She stood up "I plan to have my client plead guilty, and I will argue the sentence. You advise your clients as you please. I won't give DA Triplett his fight."

The following day in court Nancy Zimmerman stood before the court in a blue skirt, white blouse, her hair neatly combed. She heard the charges against her. She had been at the Pierce home, and was writing furiously as the other journalists were arrested. When asked how she pleads?

She softly said "Guilty."

DA Triplett was surprised, he rarely came to court, his assistants pleaded all cases. He immediately came to his feet.

"Your honor the charges which are misdemeanors warrant Mrs. Zimmerman should be punished so she, and other journalists comply with Law Enforcement officers even if they believe they are above it by hiding behind the first amendment."

Cheryl standing next to Nancy said "your honor if it please the court Mrs. Zimmeran graduated from the University of Oregon, she is employed with a prominent newspaper. She admits her mistake by pleading guilty. This is her first offence, and because she did not act quickly enough for the aggressive officers she was picked up in the frenzy."

"Your honor I object to the inflammatory language of the honorable officers who responded to the Pierce family at their request. Mrs Zimmerman did not comply with the lawful orders, and had the opportunity to leave."

"Oh save the campaign speech for the cameras. We all know this is an election year, and you are in a tough race. Please! This young lady is a first time offender who has never been in trouble, and was doing her job. She is guilty of not running off the property when ordered too!"

"I object!"

The judge banged her gavel "quiet both of you." The judge looked over her reading glasses at the young pretty journalist.

"I will impose a deferred sentence for six months. Should you come before this court Mrs. Zimmerman the entire sentence will be enforced. You will spend six months in the county jail as well as the fine on each charge. Should there be no further infractions after six months, the charges will be dropped."

The other lawyers used the same tactic. Each was given a six month deferred sentence. DA Triplett was not happy. At the Press conference he stated.

"I support Judge Mathew's decision, I may not agree; however, the sentence has been given, and I support it. I hope the journalist's understand they are not above the law. They need to respect the rights of all our citizens."

The press conference was broadcast on the local news, and picked up by the national news.

April sitting in the hospital room frowned "horse's ass."

"That's not christian" John said, looking directly at April.

"You're right as usual, I will pray for the horse's ass."

Chapter XVII

The wedding was postponed one week. Tony rested at his house being released from the hospital. Frankie, Jackie and April would travel to Tucson to prepare for the last minute details of the wedding. April self medicated with marijuana preparing for the flight to Tucson. Frank, and John would fly with Tony arriving on Thursday. Jackie helped April into the airport helping her to check in. Her eyes were glazed over, and she moved slowly. They boarded the plane convincing other passengers it would be best if they sat together since April had issues flying. She did well sitting between Jackie, and Frankie. They did their best to distract her. When the plane picked up speed lifting off April covered her face with her hands yelling, "Lord in heaven!" Frankie talked with her throughout the flight. When they landed she walked quickly off the plane pushing people out of her way as they retrieved their overhead luggage.

Tony landed at the Tucson airport. He along with John, and Frank. Jackie stood stunned as she looked at Frank. His hair was cut short. The full beard was gone, only a mustache remained. She smiled as she rubbed the smooth face.

"Thought I would make a change for Frankies wedding."

Jackie drove them to a hotel where John, and Tony stepped out. She had booked a hotel room for them, and their family. The rest of the family had arrived, and were at the hotel swimming pool. She dropped off Frank giving him instructions to go, and try on the tuxedos that had been rented. Frank frowned saying "We were all measured for the tucks, why try them on?"

Jackie stared at her husband. "You will try them on to make sure they fit!"

"Fine."

Jackie left as Frank drove to the hotel to pick up Tony, Frank, and Jordan who was Tony's best man. They arrived at the shop, and twenty minutes later sent Jackie a text. Jackie at the church decorating looked at her phone.

"I'm going to kill them all"

She handed the phone to April as Frankie looked over her shoulder. The text was a picture of the men in an odd assortment of tuxedos. Frank, and John's pants, and coats were two sizes too small. Tony had a large coat, and no pants in his boxer shorts and socks. Jordan's coat was too small, and pants too big. The coats, and pants were different colors. Some of the shirts had frills, others were plain. April stared at the photo as Frankie giggled.

Jackie sent a return message *"ALL OF YOU WILL DIE HORRIBLE DEATHS!"*

Ten minutes later she received another text. The men were in the proper tuxedos. She smiled showing April, and Frankie. She replied to the text.

"Looks better, the beatings will happen after the wedding!"

The wedding rehearsal was held on Friday evening. The wedding party went to a nice restaurant for supper. The following day all of the wedding party arrived early to take pictures. It was against tradition for the groom to see his bride in her wedding dress, however, it was decided the pictures should be taken prior to the wedding. When the pictures were taken, each went to their separate areas waiting for the wedding.

At five o'clock Frank walked into the room where Jackie, and Frankie were getting ready. He smiled "time for you to take your seat Mrs Daniels ."

She hugged Frankie walking to the front where the ushers would sit her. Frank took Frankies hand, putting her arm through his arm.

"You are beautiful."

Sissy's twins walked down the aisle dropping rose petals. Bobby's youngest son carried the pillow with the two rings on them. Tony looked at Jody who was her maid of honor. She winked at him. When the music started his heart beat fast as he saw Frank bringing Frankie down the aisle on his arm.

The wedding went well with no issues. Tony, and Frankie walked out arm in arm Husband, and Wife. They went to the VFW where the reception was held. The band was good, and as they played April looked at John "let's dance."

He frowned, but followed April to the dance floor. April could dance, and when she raised her arms and began to sway it was almost erotic. Her children sat stunned as Frankie giggled.

Tony, and Frankie ran through the line of people as they threw rice. Reaching the end of the line of people Ricky, and Bobby ran up, scooped up Frankie running to the parking lot where Roger sat in his pickup. They tossed her in as Roger spun his tires they yelled "Chivaree!"

Frank, and Jackie looked at the scene as Tony stood with his hands on his hips. John laughed looking at Frank, and Jackie as April laughed.

"Chivaree is an old custom where sometimes the bride is stolen."

The pickup returned, and as Tony walked towards it Roger sped away as Ricky, and Bobby holding Frankies arm waving them wildly yelled "Chivaree!"

Finally Roger stopped as Tony walked to the pickup. He pulled forward as Tony was near. He again pulled forward as Tony approached. The final time Ricky, and Bobby picked up Frankie as Tony walked up. They placed her in his arms. Frankie hugged his neck. He let her down, she looked at them sticking out her tongue. They ran to the pickup as Frank drove them to the airport.

TONY LIFTED OFF THE ground heading east for South Padre Island. Frankie looking at Tony asked "so what are your plans when we get to South Padre Island?"

He smiled "we will arrive in about two hours. The hotel will send a shuttle to pick us up.

I have been in space for six months. I lived with you for three weeks sleeping in a different bedroom. Watching you come out of the shower in nothing, but a towel. You sneaking into my bedroom kissing me goodnight. When we get to the hotel, I'll put the do not disturb sign on the outside doorknob, lock the door, then me, and you going to get naked!"

Frankie looked at the ring on her left hand. She giggled "That sounds like fun, now that I have a wedding ring."

the end

Don't miss out!

Visit the website below and you can sign up to receive emails whenever RB Parkline publishes a new book. There's no charge and no obligation.

https://books2read.com/r/B-A-PNYC-SWQGB

BOOKS 2 READ

Connecting independent readers to independent writers.